D0372342

Desolation Lake

Desolation Lake

a novel

Jeffrey Kwitny

Design by Meadowlark Publication Services.
Cover photos by the author.
Map on page ix © 2013 Steve Schalla. Printed with permission.
Published by Line by Line Books.
Manufactured in the United States of America.
ISBN 978-0-578-47017--7
Published 2019

For Marcella—naturally.

It is a commonplace of all religious thought, even the most primitive, that the man seeking visions and insight must go apart from his fellows and live for a time in the wilderness.

—Loren Eiseley

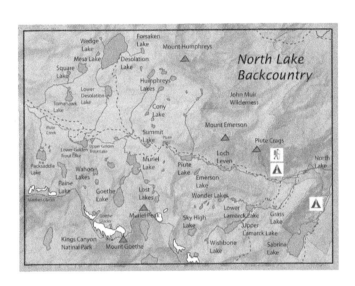

Prologue

The nightly singing of frogs always reminds me of our church's vintage organ. The old Hammond's croaking sounded soulful and had a comforting effect on me, a neglected, lonely little girl.

Within the protective womb of Saint Cecelia's Catholic Church, a haven to which they fled to temporarily escape the long misery of their marriage, my parents always sat stiffly and silently in the pews, one on each side of me like limestone sphinxes, eyes locked on the altar, unsmiling, ignoring me. Still, for a lonely kid, Sunday Masses were special. Not only did they offer a brief spell to reflect on the Gospels and the mystery of the Eucharist, which struck me as simultaneously scary and magical, they were the only occasions during which I sat in such intimate proximity to my father, who seemingly had no room in his life for human beings, especially children, and most especially me, his daughter and only offspring. A proud and vociferous atheist, a Jewish intellectual who lost his parents, his beloved sister Ruth and his faith in God to the Holocaust, my father attended those church services Sunday after Sunday, but only begrudgingly. To keep peace in the family, I suppose. To appease my mother, no doubt. I've always believed Mom's unwavering belief in sacramental Catholicism was all that kept the jagged shards of my parents' marriage glued together, like a broken heirloom vase.

Despite their pleasing, melodious signaling, I worry about them—the frogs, that is. I make my living worrying about amphibians; I work for the California Department of Forestry. I keep track of them and help keep them alive and thriving.

I wasn't always a scientist, though. I began as an English major in college—I'm deeply in love with books, whether it's classical literature or just light summer reading—but switched to science after going on a back-packing trip in the Sierras with a roommate. I found myself growing more interested, with every footstep forward on the trail, in natural phenomena as diverse as a flower's androecium or the mating habits of ecto-thermic tetrapods. As I think more carefully about it, I realize that ever since I was a small child I've turned to nature for solace. Mother Nature, the surrogate mom. The way I look at it, if Jesus of Nazareth could have a heavenly father, I see no reason for not having my own cosmic stepmom. Scientific research, I discovered later, gives me the opportunity to escape into the wilderness, where Mother Nature can cradle me in her comforting steadiness and beguile me with her myriad mysteries.

Of course, I also worry a great deal about human beings, and Edward, my husband, hasn't been sleeping well since the outbreak began.

"The problem is pandemic," he fears. "Amphibian species are experiencing severe population declines around the world," he points out to anyone who will listen, his voice growing more strident by the moment. "These are terrible times."

Let me explain. After we first arrived at the Humphreys Basin in the Kings Canyon region of the Eastern Sierras, we counted more than 8,000 tadpoles and 1,500 adult and juvenile frogs. We were studying the effects of a recent removal of non-native fish on an endangered amphibian, the *Rana muscosa.* The mountain yellow-legged frog. The little guys appeared to be thriving. But then high levels of an aquatic fungus called *Batrachochytrium dendrobatidis* entered the ecosystem, and over the course of the next four years spread across the entire watershed, dramatically reducing the frogs' population.

Then we made a discovery that changed the direction of my life. I have only to glance at the photographs of our frogs and the Eastern Sierras, beautifully framed and hanging in our study, for the details of that night and the following morning to come flooding back to me. It was then that I began believing in miracles.

As happened every work day, my husband and I, flanked on each side by the jagged peaks of Mount Humphreys and Mount Emerson, donned our field clothes, mosquito netting and waist-high rubber boots, waded into the streams trickling down from the glaciers above, conducted visual encounter surveys, marked adult frogs with pit tags, and collected field data, which we would later enter into a database and ArcGIS spatial layers that we maintained back at our home in Bishop.

It's not glamorous, the work we herps do. My husband and I labor long hours in a variety of environments and weather, and we're rarely home. By the end of each day we're covered in enflamed mosquito bites, oily sweat, water-resistant sunscreen, and snake musk. Countless times we've been bitten and scratched, spat, urinated and defecated on by the animals we work with. We don't speak much while we're working. Just the occasional "Look at this!" Still, our marriage is harmonious, even spiritual I think — we work as a team and we love each other's company. I feel just as connected to Edward and as much part of a universal scheme as the yellow-legged frogs feel a part of their habitat.

After working an especially long day of counting, measuring and classifying, Edward and I retired to our little tent, exhausted. My husband and I always share a sleeping bag. Sharing body heat can be a real advantage in certain extreme weather situations, but mostly I like the intimacy. I crawled into our sleeping bag, cozying up to my husband, expecting to doze off immediately.

Instead, as I lay wide-eyed next to him, also half-awake, I stared at the roof of our tent, about a foot and a half above our noses, listening to the sounds of nature—frogs belching drunkenly and belly-flopping in lakes, trees rustling their tresses softly in the wind—still too wound up from our toils to relinquish my hold on the day.

What stood out most were the frogs' love calls, full of longing, echoing off the walls of Mount Humphreys: usually a comforting sound that conjures up pleasant memories, as I said. Acoustic communication is essential for the frogs' survival, both in terms of defense and in localization and attraction of mates. Frogs are more often heard than seen, and we researchers rely on their friendly calls to identify them. But suddenly that night their sounds began to frighten me. The bewitched, groaning clamor, which was for frogs an expression of a need to fulfill an ancient command—to pass on their DNA and to be fruitful and increase in numbers as plentiful as the stars in the sky—suddenly sounded to me like evil spirits needing exorcising.

At last, after an hour or so of listening to their persistent, spooky pleas, I settled into the lulling limbo that lies between wakefulness and sleep. But then, just as sleep was about to finally overtake me, rain began beating in lively snare-drum syncopation on the tent's surface, quite loudly, drawing me out of my trance.

Tucked snuggly inside our polyester incubator, we were, more or less, content, considering the high volume of nature's symphony outside—until around midnight, when rainwater seeped through a small cut the size of a trimmed fingernail in the tent's skin. Icy water pooled slowly under my rolled jeans, which had served as a pillow for the past week. Our heads were encircled by this watery halo, and we dared not shift our bodies about or turn on our sides for fear of getting wet.

As I, still struggling vainly to fall asleep, listened to the rain pattering gently on the roof and the frogs calling for mates, I thought I heard—somewhere out there, deep in the wilderness, in between one frog's middle C and another's E flat, blood-chillingly sharp—a human cry for help.

The frogs suddenly stopped their raucous. The ensuing silence was troubling—it was an alarm. Bears and other predators were commonplace enough, but they would not have brought the frogs' song to a halt. We listened for a while, but there were no more human voices. It had to be the sound of the wind coursing through the canyon or possibly the cry of a hermit warbler, we reasoned. But why would the croaking stop so suddenly?

After a time, the frogs returned to their noise-making. Whatever interrupted their music had left the scene. We let it go. We were tired. We finally fell asleep.

In the morning, we crawled out of our little space-pod tent to explore the rain-soaked surroundings and satiate our curiosity, and after we ventured further into the wilderness, making our way through the maze of lodgepole pine, we discovered them.

The crumpled body of a man was draped across the legs of another man who was sitting upright with his back propped against a granite boulder the size of a baby elephant. They looked to be in their sixties, but it was hard to tell: their clothes were soaked, their hair was matted down, and they were covered in dirt. For some reason, I still remember the smell: a fusion of pine, wet clothing, and blood. They were as still as a sculpted *Pietà*. I see this image clearly in my mind even long afterward: a tableau that will never leave me.

After Edward left to find help, jogging as fast as he could down the narrow ribbon of a trail, I tended to the men. As for the man lying prostrate, rigor mortis had already set in—the hands were bent unnaturally downwards as if he were carefully picking nits from the scalp of the earth. The man sitting upright was still alive but clearly exhausted; every part of his body drooped. He appeared to be in one piece, although his face and arms were covered in enflamed scratches, and it was hard to distinguish his own blood from the other man's. He seemed unable—or unwilling—to move from his seated position against the rock face. I retrieved a

Nalgene bottle from our campsite and offered him water, which he took and drank greedily. Stopping to take a breath, he looked up and thanked me.

As we waited for help to arrive, the sun rose slowly, and Mount Humphreys looked unusually luminous to me. The thunderstorm had battered the mountain most of the night, but only a few scattered pools of rainwater, trapped in pockets of rock, provided testimony to the night's drama. The exposed boulders at the base of the mountain looked to me, in my shaken state, like the skulls of an ancient, vanquished race of giants. Blood still blotted the soil around the two men in great dark patches like colossal bruises.

Unable to move—he was clearly in terrible pain— the stranger told me his story over the course of that shimmering morning as we waited for Search and Rescue to arrive.

1

Leopold Swift, PhD., the younger of the two men who bind my story together, began each day at 4:30 in the morning by indulging in a sacred ritual: boiling water in a tea kettle; placing an unbleached paper filter in a ceramic filter cone; balancing it on a ceramic mug, purchased at the Thoreau Museum in Concord and bearing the bearded image of the author of *Walden;* measuring three heaping spoonfuls of dark roast Ethiopian coffee into the filter; pouring scalding hot water over the grounds. Making his first cup of coffee played an important part in the joyful liturgy of Doctor Swift's morning.

Leo Swift—just "Doc" or "Professor Swift" to his students. He wore round Lennon frameless glasses, anachronistic and quaint in fashion-savvy Hollywood City. His hair was mostly grey and always in disarray. He was perpetually haggard looking. His sports jacket was one size too large and made him seem as if he were about to retract into himself, like a turtle.

There was something about him that reminded people of an Old Testament prophet, Walt Whitman, or a creature from Middle-earth: the mischievous yet wise visage, the trickster temperament, the diminutive stature. Some of the older faculty members told me they believed he harked back to an aging Zonker in *Doonesbury*, while students noted a younger Gandalf. Human Resources told me he was fifty-eight but to those students who didn't get the grade they felt they deserved, he was the "old guy" English teacher who they begrudgingly admitted they were "down with." In his ratemyteacher.com reviews, students described him as "approachable," "eccentric," "passionate." "The smartest person I know." "Loves his students." "You'll learn a lot but he's not easy." "I got a 5 on the AP exam because of him." "Doc rocks!" "An Emersonian original." Another, less generously: "Awesome, except for the shitty C-plus he gave me."

Nobody knows his real name. He'd legally changed it sometime during his college years, so many of his students have testified. As he explained to his rapt audience in the classroom, "If Jimmy Gatz could change his name to Jay Gatsby, why couldn't I change mine as well? Jay Z's real name is Shawn Corey Carter, don't forget" he pointed out, and they nodded in dubious agreement. "So why can't we all reinvent ourselves?" he asked rhetorically. To his students, then, he was "Doc."

He mentioned in class that he had written his master's thesis on the dichotomy of body and soul in Jonathan Swift's works, and a doctoral dissertation on Catholic and alimentary symbolism in James Joyce's *Ulysses*. The students that'd been paying attention, the best of the senior crop, remember that he talked a lot about the duality of body and soul—it came up during the Satire Unit in his AP English Language and Composition class. His first name, Leopold, apparently another invention, was taken from Joyce's novel, or so some students have insisted.

Doctor Swift had confessed to them that he had come from a proud line of Ashkenazi Jews—grandparents from Russia and Poland, the story goes—but he had a mother whose ancestors were German Catholics from the Netherlands. He never talked about her. In fact, he never discussed his childhood at all.

He never talked about his faith either. Most assumed that because he had a PhD, he must be an atheist or at least an agnostic, like so many of his colleagues in the Lofton faculty. Nobody knew where he stood in matters of religious faith, other than what he occasionally professed to his students in the classroom: that the Golden Rule, great literary works of art, the essential goodness of his students, the sublime beauty of nature— all these things were worthy of devotion. They were causes perhaps even worth dying for.

But it was the wilderness that he loved most of all.

"In nature there is something of the marvelous," he'd tell his students, paraphrasing Aristotle.

Those few colleagues who enjoyed his company—and there weren't many, for he was antisocial, a loner who preferred to sit at his desk and correct papers rather than socialize with his colleagues—called him simply "Leo," and his ex-girlfriend knew him as Leo too, although when she was angry with him, she called him LE-O-POLD, enunciating all three syllables with irksome syncopated precision.

His only daughter, Chandler, whom he'd never met and, what's more, did not even know existed, called him no name at all. Her mother never spoke of him—at all. According to school legend, Swift's girlfriend of five years decided not to inform him that she was pregnant after he'd balked at the idea of ever getting married. He preferred the kind of romantic arrangement enjoyed by Jean-Paul Sartre and Simone de Beauvoir: free, intellectual, an open arrangement. He liked living life "on a whim," he insisted repeatedly—"making it up as I go." He preferred spontaneity and agility over tradition—"jack-be-nimble fleetfootedness," he would say. For Janice, his not believing in marriage was a deal-breaker, and she left him to have her baby without him—and without his knowledge. It was her revenge, yes. But she also had, back then (and still has), firm convictions regarding the efficacy of single-parenting.

She'd decided to have a child one way or another,

and "to hell with the self-centered bastard."

Swift taught at an elite private school known worldwide as Lofton Academy, located discreetly in the hills above a low-density residential district near the base of one side of the Santa Theresa Mountains. Near the school you'll find the trendy Aromatica Café, for instance, with its bewitching pastries and Spanish Lattes to die for. Nearby there are decaying strip malls and an equal abundance of strip clubs. Within one of these ubiquitous little malls a flashing neon light advertises a bail bondsman right next door to a Curry Bowl, which is not far from the Mathnasium Tutoring Center. The campus is also close to Hollywood CityWalk, the Lone Ranger Museum, and the Valhalla Cemetery. Contemporary pop culture, the Old West, the New SAT, the good life, crime and punishment, sin and aestheticism, death and decay—the icons of Los Angeles's schizophrenic nature.

Leo would sometimes joke with his students that, "aside from the school, the freeways, the smog, the strip malls, and the 34,000 people, if you squinted really, really hard, with your glasses off, Hollywood City provided you with an image of unspoiled nature."

Despite its meretricious surroundings, Lofton Academy was ranked by *Forbes* as one of the top prep schools in the country, and its $38,000 annual tuition "keeps the riffraff at bay," as some of the less magnanimous parents have put it. Despite the school's inescapable elitism, Doctor Swift had decided, years ago, that he would ride out his days at Lofton, considered by many members of the faculty, including himself, to be the Promised Land of Schools for teachers. It was indeed an oasis of learning in Southern California, or so many of the faculty have claimed. "A respite from the painful realities of the outside world," one teacher told me. "A kind of Castalia, like in Herman Hesse's *Glass Bead Game,* a remote place for the intellectual elite to grow and flourish," this teacher said with great pride, smiling broadly.

From what I can tell, based on my few visits to the campus to interview students and faculty, they are well-educated, friendly people, with good manners and possessing (in the case of many of the students, a dean told me with a wink) large trust funds. Leo believed that the school was a great place to teach. He considered it home. In any case, as a teacher nearing the sunset of his career, there was nowhere else for him to go.

Professor Swift sat at his desk in the English department office, where he and thirteen other teachers, ensconced in cubicles arranged in a circle around the periphery of the large room, prepared their lesson plans for the day. For Leo's juniors, it would be an introduction to American transcendentalism and its emphasis on the divinity of the natural world and all human beings. He'd constructed a PowerPoint presentation with the students' skepticism of all things spiritual in mind.

He collected his laptop, books and notepad, and

headed to class, where the best and the brightest the land had to offer awaited him. Before stepping into the classroom, he always hesitated at the threshold, for just a moment. High school students are an unpredictable species.

2

Doctor Swift smiled warmly as his American Literature students (eleventh-graders) filed into his classroom, Ruther Hall 210. He wore the same grey tweed sports jacket pretty much every day, one size too large, which made him look like a child wearing a hand-me-down, and the students sometimes liked to kid him about his conservative clothing. "Great pants, Doc!" they'd say cheerily. "Abercrombie and Finch?" His clothing was in stark contrast with the other teachers' hipster slim-fit jeans, shirts, and air-cushioned, neon-bright tennis shoes. Meanwhile, a popular chemistry teacher named Alphonse wore shorts, flip-flops, and a Hawaiian shirt every day, rain or shine.

The students never failed to greet him politely. "You look very professorial today, Doc!"

"I like to at least *look* the part. *Looking* like a professor is half the battle, right? All part of the deception," he'd always reply, with a wink. "I try to keep you guys fooled."

He welcomed his students convivially at the door, as always: "Good morning, Tamara! Ben! Lucas! How's it going, Alex?"

"Hey, Doc! I'm sorry I missed class yesterday. Did I miss anything?" This, coming from Zack Henninger, whose friendly, respectful manner always diffused all irritation. An exceptionally talented pitcher for the Academy's beloved varsity baseball team—six-foot-five, 230 pounds, he threw 100-mile-an-hour fastballs as routinely as you or I take a breath—Zack entered the classroom looking like a Greek god and acting like he was ever-aware of how his bigger-than-life image affected people: he stood erect and smiling with self-satisfaction.

"Well, Zack—it's a shame," intoned Swift playfully, with exaggerated disappointment, hoping to coax down this gentle giant from his perch on Mount Olympus. (The devil in him enjoyed stirring up a little mischief now and then.) "You see, Zack, you missed the Second Coming of Christ," he said without a trace of irony in his voice. "Tough luck, though. It was a brief visit. The Son of Man said hello and goodbye—then he left. That's it! He won't be back for another two thousand years—and *you* missed it." All this spoken with an elfish gleam in his eye. Zack blinked, his smile wavering briefly then returning brighter than ever. Zack was a fine young man, Leo knew, albeit a bit gullible, and his study skills often languished in the shallows. Zack looked beseechingly at his teacher, the joke wafting languidly over the young pitcher's head like an infield pop-up.

"Don't worry about it, Zack," said his teacher. "I was just playing with you. Just—well, if you miss class, you know I always give you and all the students a weekly schedule, and I post plans on our Axel web page. Or you can give a classmate a call. Just find out what you missed. Who knows? Maybe Sandy Koufax will pay us a visit one day you're out."

"Who?"

"Sandy—that's okay, Zack. Before your time."

Zack kept smiling. He enjoyed the attention, and he knew from experience that his teacher's teasing was a sign of endearment.

The students took their seats, arranged in a crescent facing inward, to facilitate class discussions. They waited for his lead.

Doctor Swift loved rituals—all kinds, sacred and profane: graduations, inaugurations, marriages and funerals, college rush traditions, secret meetings, sports events, Halloween and Valentine parties, gay and veterans' parades, Christmas and Easter rites, all things Catholic, replete with incense and glittering finery. He found rituals comforting in a rather dull and sometimes scary world. In the classroom, he began each study of a new literary text with a book blessing.

"The Bible is God's sacred word to man; literature is man's sacred word to God," he informed his students, solemnly, reverentially. The kids were used to their beloved teacher's little rituals, rare phenomena in this secular world, and they very much welcomed the faux benedictions. Although most of these students were proud, self-proclaimed atheists whose parents had taught them to distrust religion and worship all things trendy and consumable, they craved this sort of spirituality, simply because they were starved for an experience of the mysterious and unknowable—the reasons for existence. Children of the Enlightenment, with their feet planted firmly on the ground of rationalism, the students still needed to experience moments of transcendence: moments that would take them beyond their sensory spheres. They sometimes longed for some sense of meaning to counteract all their losses and failures.

He flicked the light switch and lowered the window drapes, plunging the classroom into sleepy half-light. Then he lit a tall white votive candle, which he kept tucked away in the top left desk drawer for these spiritual occasions, and propped it upright on the desk, using some of the melted wax to secure it.

The students' faces glowed spectrally in the flickering candlelight.

Their teacher extended his open hands over the thin book of poetry. "We ask that the Great Spirit above and the muses of all writers bless this book and bless us too. We pray that in reading Walt Whitman's and Emily Dickinson's poems we will come to have a better understanding of the workings of the human heart—of *ourselves*—and that we will become better readers, better thinkers, and—God willing—better people as well. We ask this in the name of the Over-Soul and the Eternal Truth"—and here he made the sign of the cross over the dog-eared paperback—"Amen!"

"Omayn!" they replied dutifully, replete with a Hebrew accent (he'd trained them well), synchronously—"Amen; so be it; truly."

Working in a secular school, his colleagues shook their heads knowingly whenever they caught glimpses of these classroom rituals from the hallway. His playful eccentricities were admired by some, barely tolerated by others. Classroom prayer belongs in the parochial schools, some would argue. But Swift ignored their silent contempt. (A former sixties rebel and an admirer of Emerson's *Self-Reliance,* he took some pride in his nonconformity.) In any case, his focus always remained on the students.

All those beautiful, naïve, young faces, he thought to himself as he scanned the classroom. *Mostly downcast faces, considering the poem at hand: Dickinson's "I'm nobody/ who are you?"—the frog poem—often wandering minds full of longing for such earthly concerns as what's for lunch in the cafeteria, and whose party should they attend Friday night, or far more ethereal ones such as how do they find escape from boredom and freedom from authority figures, from parents, school, country, sometimes even physical existence itself. Dickinson's rebellious outcry against conformity, inscrutable as it seems to the students at first, her little frog poem, nevertheless sneaks under the covers and cuddles with the students' anxieties, warming them, simple enough language, mischievous and playful, and yet they don't understand much of it, initially, and so I tell them to open the poem like a fine Patek Philippe watch, explore the inner workings, they should love this poem, a poem that speaks directly to adolescents, to the malcontents, to the outliers, the dorks, the geeks, and the queers, to the lonely and to the fearful, and certainly to the author, Emily Dickinson—and most of all, to me.*

3

Francine Upstead stayed home from school that day. She would miss Doctor Swift's class, which she regretted since he was her favorite teacher and the only reason to go to school. In any case, the thought of enduring another day of petty high school gossip, the insufferable teenage obsession with image and popularity, and the "existential boredom" (her words) that infected high school life—not to mention Doctor Swift's recent rejection of what he referred to as her "reductionist" claim that Emily Dickinson wrote great poems precisely because she'd remained a virgin all her life, which hurt her feelings—compelled Frannie to lie to her mother and most adults.

Lying was nothing new to her; she'd been a chronic fibber since she could remember. In any case, Frannie viewed lying as amoral rather than immoral, the act of a liberated individualist living outside the restrictions of society's "quaint sensibilities," an "artist" who subscribed to a higher, Platonic code of ethics than anything found in the Bible or the school's honor code. As she saw it, mankind's so-called morality was a by-product of natural selection, nothing more, nothing less. Unlike those "petit bourgeois moralists and backward puritans," she believed that "Art with a capital A and Love with a capital L are the only great Truths, with a capital T." And it was True that she Loved Doctor Swift.

She told her mother she thought she had a fever (the classic trick of running the thermometer under hot water before returning it to its plastic sheath always worked)—although her mother showed no real concern: one way or the other, Mom would spend the day shopping at the Beverly Center, undeterred by bothersome concerns for her daughter.

Frannie was the smartest student at Lofton. So everyone said. Her success reflected the honor of the entire school community. The student body, her teachers, the deans, administrators, parents, the maintenance staff: everybody took his or her pound of flesh, each member of the community claiming he or she had a hand in burnishing the sixteen-year-old's brilliant mind, and each one sharing in her glory, as Saturn's rings celebrated their kinship to the planet they orbited. Never mind Frannie's 4.5 GPA—that was commonplace enough in private, elite schools like Lofton. What really awed the Academy was her brilliant translation of Virgil's *Aeneid* into English, a feat she managed late at night, between one and four a.m., after she'd completed her regular homework. (She required only three hours of sleep, she claimed, and her mother rarely stepped in to remonstrate.)

But this was no mean translation. Once she'd submitted the tome to her astonished Latin teacher, who quickly realized he held in his hands a work of genius, the Academy contacted one of its numerous literary agent connections in the Alumni Association, who then forwarded the masterpiece to an agent based in New York.

Alerted to the book's greatness and to its precocious author, Penguin Classics nabbed it soon enough, and eventually it became the publisher's best-selling version of the legendary story of Aeneas. (Only Dryden's 1697 translation has outsold Frannie's book, as of this writing, followed closely behind by Robert Fagle's top-seller.)

And then, as if she'd not earned enough accolades, she won the PEN Translation Prize. Although the monetary award attached ($3,000) was not remarkably large, the award itself is considered within the academic community one of the highest honors a contemporary translator can receive.

The young woman had rightfully earned star status at the school. But Frannie wasn't just smart—she was "fucking smart," as the otherwise reserved headmaster liked to boast.

Sadly, some of the old-timers claimed Frannie was

also one of the loneliest females who had attended the school that they could remember, and these were formidable claims given the number of coeds who had graced the halls of the Academy since 1928. When her mother divorced her father, with whom Frannie apparently had an especially close relationship (at nine years old, she told her mother—defiantly interrupting one of her mother's verbal assaults on her beloved father—that she would one day marry a man just like "daddy"), she did not take it well. Already a loner, the teenager withdrew further into her world of letters: Latin ones, although she was fluent in French and Italian, and could read a little Russian as well. And then, when mom uprooted her outraged daughter and discreetly moved into an apartment, the young genius and disciple of Virgil, a writer whom she loved almost as much as her father, withdrew deeper into herself.

Her new home, the Century Tower, ensconced in what once was a backlot of a movie studio, a gorgeous, arc-shaped luxury hotel, features a 297-room tower on the north portion of the property, just off Golden Boulevard. On the thirty-second floor of that tower, Frannie ran her morning bathwater. Mom had just left. Alone in her bathroom, her visage in the bathroom mirror distorted by steam from the running bath, Frannie resembled (in her own mind) a figure in a Francis Bacon painting *(Head of a Woman V):* a grotesque, pinkish blur staring back at her. Her overall appearance reminded her of the wobbly runt in a litter of puppies, the one that the canine mother instinctively gobbled up to rid the gene pool of a failed parturition.

The faint odors of spawning mildew, stale towels, and a neglected toilet (her mom barred the maid service from intruding on their privacy during her period of mourning) enhanced Frannie's feeling that life was indeed a living hell—"Death in Life," as Doctor Swift had put it, quoting from Coleridge.

Her teachers, like her mom, were oblivious to all this suffering, of course; she kept her feelings to herself. The faculty knew her only by her work, and that was always exemplary. As far as they were concerned, she was an outstanding student, possessing an impressive work ethic and a brilliant mind. The deans dutifully emailed the faculty, informing them of the divorce—but at a prestigious, topflight school like Lofton, a school situated at the heart of the film capital of the world, divorces were unexceptional. Few gave it a second thought, other than her dean, perhaps, and some of her teachers. But no one cried for this young woman. No one except her favorite teacher, Leopold Swift.

4

The last day Leo saw Frannie was the Thursday before the big announcement. She'd missed a week of school, and her dean was deeply concerned.

It was during lunch, and the quad was teeming with students clumped together in their little cliques, some climbing the steps to the library in pairs, others meeting to share gossip in the restrooms, filing in and out of the cafeteria like seed-harvesting ant species in the genera *Messor*, *Pheidole* and *Pogonomyrmex*, carrying their trays heaped with adolescent treasure: fried chicken, teriyaki chicken, tostadas, French fries, white rice, macaroni and cheese.

He spotted her sitting cross-legged on the ground next to the Japanese Privats lined up like tin soldiers behind the English building, reading. She was alone, as always. Propped between her legs, a thick book held her attention. Leo approached her cautiously; he hated to break her trance. Still, he couldn't help hearing

Dickinson's imagined voice in his head: *"I'm nobody. Who are you?"*

She looked up only after he spoke: "Hello, Frannie!" he said, rather too cheerfully, and when there was no answer, "Whatcha reading?"

Because the sun was positioned in the sky behind his head, she squinted, making her look confused—then she smiled broadly. "Oh, hi, Doctor Swift."

"Want some company?" Leo asked delicately, unwilling to trespass into hallowed space—her well-guarded privacy.

"Of course," she said, still smiling.

He crouched facing her, surveying the grass cautiously before sitting down. "I don't mind grass stains," he explained. "It's washing machines that I loathe." Her sustained smile was welcoming. "What's this?" he asked, indicating the book in her lap.

"Tolstoy. Война и миръ, *Voyna i mir,*" she said in authentically accented Russian. *War and Peace.* "What strikes me, even more than the realism of the battle scenes, is the psychological realism. Napoleon's mega-lomania is palpable, and the confusion and panic of the soldiers on the battlefield is anything but romanticized. Cannonball disembowelments are shocking, as they should be. It reminds me of the imagery depicting the horrors of war in the *Iliad.*"

"You really are an amazing person, Frannie, you know that? You'd make a fine English or classics professor," he said admiringly. He looked nervously around. He felt a twinge of panic: he feared getting too close to his students and the potential consequences of teacher-student intimacy, and he knew he must choose his words carefully. *The Thought Police are everywhere.*

"I'm only a junior in high school," she laughed. "Why would I be worrying about a career? I'm just a kid," she added coyly, as if this fact dismayed her. In fact, she knew well enough she was Ivy League-bound.

"Yes, of course that's true," he said and tried to smile back at her. "Just a kid indeed."

"I just want to get through this day," she said, suddenly looking terribly serious.

"Frannie. You're a good person, a *wonderful* person."

"My whole life—" she started to say, but caught herself.

He placed a hand gently on her left knee, which extended out to him from the cross of legs. "It's all going to be okay," he said comfortingly. "Really and truly."

She nodded, looking down at the open pages in her lap.

"I'm telling you, Frannie. Whatever is troubling you, you'll get through it."

She smiled back at him, her mouth twisting into an indecipherable, jagged line, like a tear in fabric.

5

When Frannie finally showed up for class, late as usual, she looked troubled, pensive. The other students had had a roundtable discussion on the topic of the role of punctuation in Dickinson's poetry—her beloved dashes in particular—that went well enough. The students loved arguing over interpretive material like this since it meant there were no right or wrong responses, only theoretical ones, and that meant they could not be wrong—at least, not most of the time. Anyway, Dickinson was dead and couldn't deny any of their claims, even the far-fetched ones.

"Say what you like," he often told them reassuringly. "You're free to say whatever you like here—as long as you are respectful of others' views. That's the *only* rule here."

Frannie lingered after class, when both she and her favorite teacher had an X period.

"I'm glad you came to class today," Leo said in all

earnestness once the other students had cleared the classroom, his friendly smile meeting and neutralizing her nervous stare. She stood there awkwardly, shifting her weight from side to side.

"I know you understand Dickinson," he said. "The speaker in her poem refers to herself as a Nobody. There are many "nobodies" here on campus."

Frannie looked up again and met his gaze. "Dickinson capitalizes the common noun Nobody," she said, encouraged by his smile. "Others meant it to mean 'loser' or some other dismissive insult. She makes it a proper noun, a proper name. She wears the title, spoken pejoratively by the Somebodies, like a badge of honor."

"Yes. Well put."

"The way I see it," she said confidently, "Dickinson's speaker, who thinks of the Somebodies as an 'admiring bog,' a bunch of croaking, self-admiring morons, thinks of herself as above it all—'above the fray,' as they say. Is she prideful? Isn't that the key question? Probably. But she lives on, and she's managed to bond with a fellow freak."

Perhaps it was simply a matter of reckless abandon, or his persistent preference for living life on a whim. For whatever reason, Leo stood and faced Frannie, who was now suddenly at a loss for words as she watched him expectantly, like the toddler waiting for the hug, or something more, and he spoke perhaps unwisely but nevertheless from the heart: "That's what I like about you, Frannie. We're a lot alike. I've always thought of myself as one of the nobodies."

Their eyes met and then words erupted from the girl's mouth like an unexpected and explosive series of spasmodic sneezes: "Then there's two of us. I think you're great, Professor Swift. And I love you!" Her eyes then brimmed with tears, and she apologized, sputtering, "I'm sorry! I'm so sorry!"

He looked quickly at the door. He was horrified. Closed. When did that happen? Who closed it? A student passing by the room? Another teacher? Had he mistakenly thought it was open when actually it wasn't, distracted as he was? No. Not a chance. He'd left it open, he was certain of that. He knew better. He was always careful. He always left the door open. Reflexively. His mentor, Jerry Hinckle, had warned Leo when he began teaching at Lofton about leaving classroom doors open. One-on-one meetings with students in private invite speculation, and trouble.

Nevertheless, he'd made a critical mistake.

Leo grabbed the knob and yanked open the door, blustered headlong, making it worse: "Frannie, I'm your *teacher*. I'm not who you think I am."

"I'm sorry!" she cried out, it was more like a wail this time, and she scooted off the desk, grabbed her backpack from the floor, and dashed out of the room. Several students and two of his colleagues in the English department, Ariana Clemly and Charlie Grossfit, watched open-mouthed as Frannie ran down the hall and out of the building, sobbing, clearly distraught, manic even, without once looking back.

When he read the email she'd sent late that night—was it midnight?—asking to meet with him in the morning, anywhere, to clarify, to renounce, to justify, he responded in the manner of the cool, dispassionate professional: he suggested that Francine drop by the English department office—in the company of his colleagues—on Friday morning. He received no response.

6

When Doctor Swift sat at his desk on Friday, he began his work day by fulfilling a second cherished ritual. He began by removing his laptop from its case and opened it, placing it squarely on his desk. Then he visited the teachers' break room down the hall, where he fetched his usual half-cup of jet-black, caffeine-rich Peet's coffee, bringing it back to his desk in his cherished blue coffee mug, emblazoned with the word *Walden,* the one given to him as a Christmas gift from his favorite student, Francine Upstead.

Sipping the scalding liquid judiciously, savoring its smoky, burnt taste, which always reminded him of backwoods campfires, Leo pressed the power button on the aging Dell laptop before him, and waited patiently for the machine to boot. The coffee seemed especially bitter that day; his colleague Chuck Hitchcock had no doubt added an extra spoonful to the coffeemaker filter that morning.

Leo's mail popped onto the laptop's screen. At the top of the list was an email from the headmaster to the entire faculty and staff. Leo scanned the notification, but only a few words registered:

> *It is with great and shared sorrow that I inform you of the death of Francine Upstead '17. Frannie, a beloved student, friend and daughter ... passed away yesterday evening after falling from a Century Court Tower apartment building ...*
>
> *There will be a special assembly held Monday in Templar Gym at 8.*

Leo sat at his desk, staring blankly at the screen, the world utterly stilled. Sometimes, for Leo, the heavenly machinations of God were terrifying.

7

After the news of Frannie's death had spread to the far reaches of the Lofton community, Leo drove north with a vengeance—even maniacally, some might say—to the westernmost edge of Los Angeles County, where the long spine of the mountains passed into Ventana County: the Santa Theresa Mountains National Recreation Area. There, the waters that flow into Cheeseboro and Palo Comado canyons begin their journey to the Pacific.

Wearing his dusty Merrell hiking boots and a wide-brimmed hat, Leo trekked to Sulphur Springs and then to the top of Scenic Peak, two and a half hours from the trailhead. He walked briskly. Stopping to catch his breath, he viewed this corner of the world and looked down on the small community known as Oak Village that he'd left behind.

He walked alone, quietly, hoping to avoid disturbing the local fauna along a narrow trail amid the dry grasses and the valley oaks that reach truly majestic proportions in this region, with trunks as much as six or seven feet in diameter. To Leo they presented a graceful appearance on the landscape, widely spaced with branches that sometimes draped elegantly over to lightly touch the ground, like Victorian women's skirts. The trees were reassuring in their age and toughness. *Time cools, time clarifies,* he told himself as he plodded along. He knew the story of the Chumash, who lived in these canyons for thousands of years. Many trails within the canyons most likely originated with the Chumash and then were expanded by the ranchers who followed. The native plants, exposed to heavy grazing and unable to adjust, were replaced with European mustard and thistles. Native plants were not the only things affected, however, by the onslaught. Grizzly bears, once thriving in the canyons, were exterminated by the ranchers.

When he arrived at the half-mile-high summit of the highest peak in the range, Leo slipped his pack off his shoulders and let it drop to the ground. He looked heavenward. The sun was high in the sky and bright, and its rays warmed his face.

He then looked down at the earth. Digger bees—ground nesting insects that seem to like the semi-compacted soil along the margins of trails—circled a hole in the ground near his boots. The diggers looked to him like fuzzy honeybees.

Leo shrugged off his day pack, unzipped it, found the Nalgene water bottle, and took a swig. He surveyed the land. As the sun dropped behind the mountain, throwing a shadowy blanket over the canyon, Leo reluctantly made his way back to his car. He knew that it was dangerous to walk alone in the canyon after dark; more than forty-five mammal species can be found in these mountains, ranging in size from shrews, which weigh less than an ounce, to 150-pound mountain lions. But it was the rangy, hungry-eyed coyotes that made him especially nervous.

The sun dropped to the west, and Swift dutifully followed it. In the purple light, with Edward Hopper shadows lengthening and consuming him, Swift looked to the sky for answers.

A solitary red-tailed hawk circled above, making a halo over him the circumference of the Century Court Tower roof.

For the bird with the brick-colored tail, breeding season had passed, and the fall breezes brought a faint chill to the proceedings. Leo wished his airy companion had a mate. Breeding season initiates a spectacular sequence of aerial acrobatics, and Swift wanted to watch the birds' Cirque du Soleil–like spectacle.

Hawk pairs fly in large circles. They gain great height before the male plunges into a vertiginous dive and makes a steep climb back to circling height to join his mate. Later, the birds lock talons and freefall spiraling toward earth. It was a beautiful love-making ritual that was mesmerizing to Leo.

This lonesome red-tail's day of hunting had come to an end. He suddenly broke away from his circular pattern and his wings beat against the Santa Anas, sometimes known as the "devil winds," carrying him away and away into the direction of the setting sun, and Leo Swift followed his lead.

8

After returning his daypack to the car trunk, where he always kept his hiking gear—boots, backpack, tent, all the trekker's paraphernalia that enabled him to go backpacking on a whim—he drove through the Santa Theresa Mountains on a windy canyon road on his way to the beach.

The sparkling, diamond-dappled surface of the Pacific always managed to startle Leo as he rounded the last curve and the spectacle unfolded before him. It was such a clear afternoon that he could make out Catarina Island in the distance, ephemeral in the bright light, resting like a dog sleeping blissfully on the horizon line.

At the first intersection he encountered, Swift noticed that a line of cars—heavy traffic was rare on this stretch of road—was making its way out of the parking lot of the local Catholic church. Traffic was backed up all the way to the Golden Coast Highway. What was the church's name? He hadn't visited this local landmark—the L.A. Archdiocese's remotest outpost of the faith—in years. Who was the pastor? Was Monsignor McGillis—was that his name?—still delivering those intricate, mazelike sermons on the Real Presence of Christ in the Eucharist?

Guilty survivor, shaken to his soul. *Child killer. Guilty as charged.* Where do you go when all is lost? He parked the car two blocks from the church and made his way up the street.

The Reverend Father Thomas Branimir Gerbajs, *Ordo Fratrum Praedicatorum,* walked out of the church to the parking lot, where a colossal tent had been pitched and seven hundred parishioners, clergy, and religious from the far corners of the archdiocese, civic officials, interfaith church leaders, relatives, and longtime friends gathered for the funeral Mass of Irish-born Monsignor Timothy Cianán McGillis, pastor emeritus. Father Tom stood behind the temporary podium erected in the old NO PARKING corner of the lot, the microphone arched in a comma to his face—a grey-bearded, wolf-like visage. Like so many liturgical and church-related events, the service had a theatricality to it that injected high drama into the proceedings.

As Father Tom read from his notes, his amplified voice was occasionally punctuated by electronic whistling feedback.

"Cardinal Ronald McCovey, Archbishop Adolfo Ramirez, members of the clergy, parishioners, family, friends and neighbors. Brothers and sisters. At his baptism, Timothy Cianán McGillis died and was buried with Christ, only to rise with him to the newness of life."

An experienced homilist, keenly aware of the importance of controlled rhetoric, of dramatic effect and timing, he paused before continuing, looking at the sea of loving faces.

"Let us ask ourselves, what is the great Truth that Jesus knew? What great Truth did the Son of God know that Monsignor McGillis had learned, thanks to the Holy Spirit? A truth that attracted to the Monsignor the powerful and the meek, the saint and the sinner, the brightest lights and the fading lights? What is the great Truth that was revealed to Timothy McGillis that enabled all of us to feel hallowed in his presence? To feel as if we were valuable and loved? To genuinely feel that each one of us was his best friend? This is what he knew: life is a gift from God. And the only proper response is one of complete and utter gratitude."

Somewhere in the transfixed crowd, a solemn and reverential field of faces, Leo Swift nodded in silent approbation.

9

Father Tom listened to confessions Saturday afternoons. This sturdy church, his home since 1996—built in 1950, the Hall and the Rectory in 1953, and the school in 1954—buttresses a hillside overlooking the Pacific. In the confessional, there is a screen and a kneeler. Placed on the kneeler is a plaque with the Act of Contrition written on it.

Father Tom was waiting in the small compartment when Leo entered.

"Peace be with you," said the priest.

"Hello, Father," Leo began. "Um … Although I was raised Catholic, I'm not exactly sure what I'm supposed to do."

Father Tom leaned in closer to the grill. "New to our parish?"

"I haven't been to mass since I was a kid."

"Okay. Not a problem. Glad to have you back!"

"It's been easily fifty years."

"So. Then. What can I do for you?" asked the priest in his best welcoming voice.

"I've done bad things, really terrible things."

"Oh, my. Yes, indeed. Well then. You truly are a member of the human race. Go to Heaven for the climate, Hell for the company, the saying goes," he said cheerily.

Leo looked closer at the grate separating the two men.

"Sorry. I was quoting Mark Twain. The man's a national treasure." Clearing his throat, he returned to a more appropriately somber tone. "You were saying? Tell me what, exactly, is preventing you from experiencing the fullness of life?"

The interior of the confessional was shadowy dark, and the grill prevented him from seeing his confessor, but Leo could sense that the man cared. It was the tone of the voice. Consoling. He'd used it himself, many times, in the classroom.

"What do you do for a living?" continued the priest.

"I'm a teacher at a school not far from here. I teach high school English. Juniors and seniors."

"That's wonderful!"

"It *is* wonderful. Lofton truly is a wonderful school. Great teachers. Great kids. There is one student, a brilliant girl ..." This wasn't going to be easy, and so he chose his words carefully, as if every syllable meant life or death. "She was the brightest student I've ever known, maybe the school's ever known" he continued, "and … we'd chat sometimes, for thirty or forty-five minutes at a time, right after class. About literature mostly. About philosophy. Life." He then added tentatively: "I think she had a crush on me."

"I'm sure it happens a lot in your profession."

"She told me she loves me."

"Oh."

"I encouraged her to share her worries and thoughts with me. I wanted to encourage her as much as possible, this amazing prodigy. And then one day … one day she tells me she loves me." His voice fell to a whisper.

"I see," said Father Tom sighing deeply. "That really *is* a problem. How did you handle it?"

"Well, I was stunned of course. I didn't know what to say. This had never happened before. But I was rather hard-hearted about it, I think. It was like—I became all business. All professional. Cold as hell, really." The words were pouring forth now. "I said nothing, did nothing, pretended it never happened. I should have consulted with my department chair, or someone in admin, or maybe called her mother … *someone*. Instead, I kept it to myself. Did nothing. Not a goddamn thing. I was hard as a rock. And truthfully? I don't know why. I don't understand this side of myself. The cold side. The Mister Hyde side."

"Your students no doubt look up to you. You're not only a teacher, but a friend, a wizened philosopher, a surrogate parent for some of those kids. You have a passion for teaching, which they *sense* — a profound *love* of your subject, of books, a love for working with young people —"

"Even when her parents broke up," Leo interrupted, impassioned, "she never emailed me, never came by the office … never asked for anything … and I did nothing, not even then. Even when I knew that her parents' divorce was killing her."

"And so you feel like you let her down, is that right?"

"Yes. I *did* let her down."

"I understand completely. Letting people down can be a terrible thing, especially when you care about them."

"I withdrew, Father. From Janice, my ex-girlfriend, then from this student — Frannie. Both times, closed myself right off."

"Okay. All right"

"And then, about a week ago, I found out she'd committed suicide." He heard an intake of breath from the other side of the partition. "The newspaper said she'd jumped from an apartment building."

Then, cutting through the thick fog of self-loathing that shrouded Leo in the dim, claustrophobic space of the confessional, a reaching voice: "You are no doubt a good man," said the priest. "I can sense that. And you have taken on a prodigious and terrible measure of guilt. You've been carrying on your shoulders a very, *very* heavy cross indeed."

Father Tom waited for a response. The penitent had nothing more to say.

"Okay, my friend," the priest continued. "I want you to consider doing a few things. First, you need to reach out to the girl's family, and do the right thing with your employer. I'm also going to ask you to attend mass beginning this Sunday. Second, memorize the Lord's Prayer, if you don't already know it. And be sure to say it every day, without fail—when you're alone and when it's quiet. Jesus said, *When you pray, enter into your room and when you have shut the door, pray to your Father which is in secret*—Matthew, Chapter Six, verses five and six. Third, I want you to thank God for all your blessings—especially the gift of life—bestowed on you. Count them—your blessings. One by one. Every day. The number will most certainly grow in time, if you pay enough attention. Then, in perhaps a month, let's continue our dialogue. But start with the prayer."

Leo nodded and remained silent.

"And be sure to count your blessings. Every single day!"

Father Tom closed with a prayer:

"God, the Father of mercies, through the death and resurrection of His Son, has reconciled the world to Himself and sent the Holy Spirit among us for the forgiveness of sins;

through the ministry of the Church may God give you pardon and peace, and I absolve you from your sins in the name of the Father, and of the Son, and of the Holy Spirit."

Leo thanked the priest and stepped out of the tiny booth. There was no one else waiting and the church was empty except for the kind confessor, who remained in the confessional. Still feeling guilty and hating to abandon this benevolent person who'd listened patiently to his confession and with whom he'd shared this private shame, he turned toward the entrance.

He stopped to gaze at the mahogany crucifix hanging on the wall behind the altar table, a hand-carved image of Christ hanging limply, as if all the muscles in his emaciated body had been lengthened in an exaggerated manner by the sculptor.

The wooden corpus: collapsed, beautiful, bony, and desolate.

10

Leo returned to his 426-square-foot studio apartment. A half block from Ventana Boulevard, less than a mile from the CityWalk, it was an easy drive to Lofton. With air conditioning; a balcony the size of a card table; cable for his 32-inch conventional, non-HD TV; a rattling dishwasher; a serviceable microwave oven; a miniature closet, a washer and dryer—the apartment provided Leo, a simple man with simple needs, with everything a bachelor requires.

He counted his blessings, as Father Tom had instructed him. He had:

✓ his health;
✓ a job he loved, devoted to the honorable cause of teaching young people to read and write better;
✓ a roof over his head and food and his table;

✓ his hikes in the Santa Theresas and in the
   Sierras;
✓ Italian opera, and Puccini in particular;
✓ books—his beloved books;
✓ life itself.

And yet, despite this formidable list of blessings, there was this persistent …

The silence of the apartment absorbed all further thought. Leo crossed over to the kitchen counter and tapped the button on his CD player. Eyes closed, he listened to the music that filled the apartment and uplifted his heart: the "Nessum Dorma" aria from Puccini's *Turandot*. Healing beyond just the words, a healing only music can perform.

It is the final act, and Calaf is alone in the moonlit palace gardens. He hears, in the distance, Turandot's messengers proclaiming her command. The aria begins with a reflection on the lovely princess:

Nessun dorma! Nessun dorma!
Tu pure, o Principessa, nella tua fredda stanza,
guardi le stelle che tremano d'amore,
e di speranza!

None shall sleep! None shall sleep!
Even you, o Princess, in your cold bedroom,

watch the stars that tremble with love
and with hope!

Pavarotti's voice radiated a gorgeously warm romantic glow around Leo, a cocoon of light and sound. The singing has an unforced, open-throated quality, which Italians call *lasciarsi andare*—letting it pour forth—a voice that Leo treasured.

He opened his eyes. Two images caught his attention. Having been a hiker and backpacker for more than ten years, having explored a healthy chunk of the Eastern Sierras and much of the Santa Theresas, he'd learned a little about ornithology, so he recognized immediately the bird roosting on his open window sill: a common mourning dove.

Signs and symbols were honored by English teachers and mystics alike.

Then Leo shifted his gaze to the letter in his daily pile of junk mail that included advertisements from Vons, Trader Joe's, and a company named Hi-Five Re-Fi pushing something about refinancing home mortgages. Opening the envelope, Swift took out the handwritten letter and read:

Dear Dad—

His eyes locked on the second word. He had no children of his own; he'd made certain of that when he severed his relationship with Janice. That was the main reason for their breakup twenty years ago: she wanted children and he didn't—at least not then. Simply put, he was too afraid. The prospect of marriage and children was a deal-breaker for Janice. At thirty-five, she believed that there were two reasons God had placed her on earth: first, to be a nurse and help those who were suffering from disease, and second, to fulfill her biological imperative of bringing children of her own into the world. She pressed him one last time about the issue and when he hesitated to respond correctly—a fatally long, twelve-second hesitation—their relationship quickly unraveled like a pair of shoelaces. He found himself tripping over every meal conversation, and when she entered their bed at night, she turned her back on him—there was to be no reconciliation through lovemaking.

When she'd met Leo, he seemed so promising; the moment augured well for the future. He had a doctorate in English. He had a sense of humor: they were talking outside the café when a bird discharged its waste directly overhead and a white blob landed in his hair. Instead of losing his dignity, he contorted his face into a grimace and said something about a superstitious belief that if a bird poops on you, your car, or your property, you may receive good luck and riches. "Pennies from heaven," he added in a sage voice. That was then.

Janice had waited until her partner of five years (a length of time that had tested her patience beyond

all reason) had left for work. She packed her belongings—the important stuff, such as her mother's pearl
necklace and a few changes of clothes, all in all filling
a mere two suitcases—and left, never to return.

Maybe they were—or could have been—mates.
Literary examples abound. Heathcliff and Cathy. Jay and
Daisy. Quasimodo and Esmeralda. Jane and Rochester.
Mr. Darcy and Elizabeth.

She was six weeks pregnant when she left him.

When Swift arrived home that afternoon, he found
her goodbye letter, read it, and howled. *I am banished!* he
thought. And that was the last time he heard from Janice.

So, then, what in the world did this "Dear Dad"
mean?

> *Dear Dad,*
> *I know you're not really my dad but I like to think*
> *of you as one. I don't know if you are aware of this,*
> *but my biological dad is out of the picture, and my*
> *mom is an alcoholic.* A fronte praecipitium a tergo
> lupi. *I failed to tell you this after I left your English*
> *class, but if it weren't for you, I would never have*
> *fallen in love with literature. You are my favorite*
> *teacher and my favorite human being. You opened*
> *my eyes and my curiosity. But mostly you opened*
> *my heart. To paraphrase Ralph Waldo Emerson,*
> *you turned my inside out and my outside in. I just*
> *wanted to make sure you knew how much I appreciate*

everything and how much I love. And now, Acta est
fabula, plaudite!

*With eternal love, your fellow Nobody (but don't
worry, there's a pair of us!),*
Frannie

Her words went through him like something lethal.
He tried to imagine what it was like falling from the
balcony of a twenty-eight-story apartment building.
Would you be conscious of your falling on the way
down? Would you pass out from terror? Would you
die instantly upon impact?

His heart was pounding vitriol through him. He
wanted to scream like a banshee. Instead, what came
out sounded amphibian. He'd only cried twice in his
life, as far as he could remember: the first when he was
in high school and reading Steinbeck's *Of Mice and Men,*
after George shot his best friend, Lenny; the second
was when he learned during a telephone call from his
mother that his father had died. And now …

All he could do was cradle his face in his arms and
croak.

11

Leo's Honda Civic crawled along Holly Canyon Boulevard, traffic already backed up for miles in the morning rush hour. Time to think before entering a classroom. Time to try out a prayer: not improvised but an ancient meditation, in words many believe the Word, the Son of Man, had taught his own students 2,000 years ago. Alone, with the windows rolled up securely against the roar of passing cars, he practiced the Lord's Prayer, as Father Tom had requested.

Once ensconced safely at his assigned space in the faculty parking lot, his name painted in white on the dusty grey asphalt, Leo stepped out of his car—modest compared to the BMWs, Audis, the occasional Mustang convertible, Range Rovers, and two or three Teslas that crowded the student parking lot—crossed the quiet, mostly deserted grounds, and mounted the steep flight of stairs leading up to Ruther Hall.

Once at his desk, he began his daily work ritual,

interrupted momentarily by a vision outside the window: wild daffodils in the narrow space between the building and a fence, brilliant in the morning light, cloud-cover soft.

Before the first coffee of the day, he checked his voice mail. First up was a message from the dean of faculty who asked if he would be so kind as to pay him a visit in his office—before first period would be perfect. *Not good,* he thought. He left his lesson plan half finished; he needed the time to prepare. It wasn't the first time the well-meaning administration had shackled his ability to do his job well.

All he wanted to do was get back to his teaching.

12

To Leo, Aaron Chestfaller still looked like a student at Lofton even though he was forty-three. He would eternally resemble a seventeen-year-old model, with shiny golden locks carefully parted and brushed to one side, despite twenty years in various administrative positions following graduation from Lofton and four years at Stanford, where he'd earned a master's in education. Leo wondered if the sequestered world of Lofton, with its endless ebb and flow of students and teachers, preserved life somehow. *Was Gatsby right,* he wondered, *about the appeal of upper-class life with its "breathless air," its offering of immortality, a heavenly realm "safe and proud above the hot struggles of the poor"?* Leo wanted to remain left alone, sequestered, a literary monk, a fly in amber.

Chestfaller pointed to an empty chair.

"Leo," he said, and tried to smile at Leo but it came off unintentionally as a smirk.

"Aaron." Leo waited without saying anything further.

Chestfaller leaned back in his chair and rested his hands on his chest. Everything was revealed in his face. He looked sad. The details gave him away: the beads of sweat on Chestfaller's forehead. He made his face smile.

"Thanks for stopping by, Leo," he said, holding the smile with visible difficulty. "I've got a meeting I've got to get to, so I'll be quick about this."

"What's up, Aaron?" Leo said worriedly. He noticed a handwritten letter on the desk. Chestfaller snatched the crinkled slip of and held it with trembling fingers before him — his shield of Achilles.

"Well, I've got a problem," he said, suddenly losing his smile, which was replaced with a look that was difficult to decipher — perhaps it was confusion.

Meaning I've got a problem, knew Leo. He silently recited the first thing that came to mind:

Our Father, who art in heaven, hallowed be thy name …

"This is a political matter, nothing personal. The school isn't accusing you of anything."

"Accusing me? This is about Frannie Upstead, isn't it?"

"Her aunt is on the Board of Trustees, as you may know."

"I didn't. I thought only the wealthiest parents — the ones with power, the lawyers, CEOs headed the board." He considered running like as rabbit, bolting for the door, but closed his eyes and remained in his chair. He continued with the prayer in his mind:

… thy kingdom come, thy will be done …

Uncomfortable, squirming visibly, Chestfaller forged ahead. "The aunt is rather well to do. It didn't hurt that Frannie came from the Fontaine School and had the highest ISEE scores of any of our candidates, of course." With this, Chestfaller's spine became erect— again, the school pride, as if somehow Lofton had something to do with her brilliance. At best the school succeeded in providing just enough kindling to keep the flames of her intellectual furnace stoked.

"Tell me exactly, what's up, Aaron. I have to go to class in exactly twenty-eight minutes," said Leo with irritation beginning to creep into his voice.

Chestfaller raised the letter a foot higher in the air. He looked like the Statue of Liberty holding her torch. "Frannie wrote this letter before the suicide. It's a love letter."

Leo froze.

… on earth as it is in heaven …

To be fair, Chestfaller looked genuinely crestfallen. "It doesn't look good and—"

Leo's eyes flashed a look of desperation. "Wait a minute." Leo spoke consciously, pleadingly. "I did nothing inappropriate."

… give us this day our daily bread …

Leo went on. "I talked with her about literature,

philosophy, all sorts of subjects, usually right after class." He squeezed his eyes shut.

... and forgive us our trespasses, as we forgive those who trespass against us ...

"I believe you, Leo," he replied.

Leo opened his eyes, newly inspired. "Teachers have befriended their students since antiquity. Think Socrates and Alcibiades. Think Anne Sullivan and Helen Keller."

"That's true. You're absolutely right, Leo."

"Okay, then." Leo stood up and looked at the clock. 7:33. "Can I go?"

"The issue is that the aunt—mind you, she's a former prosecutor, rich as hell, and a bit of a royal pain in the ass, to be frank—she gives massive donations to the school's endowment."

"And?"

... lead us not into temptation ...

"And there's something else."

Leo waited, one hand resting on the door knob.

"Remember last year's Crab Fest—"

Leo focused fixedly on the dean. "It was fairly uneventful, as school parties go."

"There were members of the faculty who acted and spoke, uh, freely, and perhaps with a little inappropriateness that night. Typical of these things."

Leo glanced once more at the clock; the second hand seemed to have slowed.

"One faculty member shared a story with me, Leo.

In fact, several teachers spoke to me. I guess the alcohol loosened more than a few tongues."

Leo stared at him. "Whose tongues? About what?"

"Doesn't matter. Several of your colleagues said you were sitting on the grass behind Ruther Hall. With Frannie Upstead. They said it was just the two of you, and that you had your hand on her leg—"

"Aaron! What are you talking about?"

"It was reported. They *saw*."

"I'm telling you—"

"They saw what they saw. The sighting was corroborated by several of the faculty."

"Frannie was a lonely girl. I shared my time with her. I tried to be a friend. But *nothing happened!*"

"As you probably already know, there's a zero-tolerance policy at all the schools regarding this sort of thing, Leo, especially with all the child-abuse scandals tearing apart the L.A. Archdiocese and half of L.A. Unified."

Leo stood shaking.

"Anyway, it came up at the trustees' meeting. Frannie's aunt is looking for a scapegoat for her niece's death. She's out for someone's head. *Your* head, I'm afraid to say. You understand, there's no way she'll accept that her sister's divorce, *or* her bad parenting, had anything to do with Frannie's suicide."

... but deliver us from evil ...

Chestfaller returned the letter to a manila folder and

refiled it carefully, as if it were ancient papyrus rather than milled paper, in a lower desk drawer. He sighed audibly. Then, hoping to win Leo over, he continued in a facetious tone, "Obviously her sister couldn't be a fuckup of a mother, which we all know she was, she had nothing to do with her niece's death, right? We all know that's how they think."

"Right."

"So she wants you out. And she'll skin you alive if necessary. You're to be drawn and quartered, metaphorically speaking."

"It's. All. Wrong," was all Leo could articulate.

"With all the news media frothing at the mouth like rabid dogs, looking for another Lofton scandal—"

"We were *friends*, Aaron," Leo offered quietly. "That's it."

"—and with Myra Glick out for blood—"

"Aaron …"

"Ron wants you to take a leave of absence, Leo—while HR conducts an investigation. Anyway, Commencement is only a few weeks away."

Leo nodded, looked down at his hands. Then at the clock.

7:44.

"It's a game Ron feels he has to play," said Chestfaller, a new flatness modulating his voice. "For now, anyway. You'll be back in in the fall, I'm sure. Give it the summer."

Leo felt a growing numbness spread from his toes to his scalp as if he were an etherized patient. He reached for the doorknob. "I've got to get to class."

"Don't worry about it," said Chestfaller, standing. "I spoke to your department chair. He's got people covering your classes from now until final exams. Substitutes we brought in."

Leo looked genuinely stormed, keeled, and sunk as he stood there silently.

… For thine is the kingdom, the power, and the glory, now and forever.

13

Rumors instantly radiated in all directions about the scandal striking the prestigious and newsworthy Lofton Academy, the "Prep School of the Stars," as some headlines called it. It took no time before the blogosphere was erupting like Vesuvius with rumors and speculation—not for attribution—on Doctor Swift's administrative leave. The story even made ABC's evening news. In response, the headmaster, Ronald Lubitsky, sent out an email to the entire school community—faculty and staff, students and parents—that expressed the Academy's position.

I cannot emphasize enough how important it is to all of us at Lofton that we protect our students. For this reason, we are committed to carrying out our investigation in a thorough and fair manner. To this end, we have hired Godfrey Lancaster, a partner at the law firm of Tettinger, Rojels & Garesty, to lead our investigation. Lofton's board is forming a special committee to oversee the investigation.

It was a Saturday morning, and Leo was returning from the store with groceries in the trunk. As he turned the corner, he slowed to a crawl, then pulled into a parking space. Two sheriff's patrol cars and a police van were parked outside his apartment building. Officers entered and exited like Australian yellow crazy ants carrying dead insects and seeds. But those weren't items from nature, they were his belongings—there went his laptop. The squad went about divesting his apartment of his possessions, and Leo wanted to leap out of his car and block their paths, but he sat immobilized, watching the nightmare scene as if it were a low-budget horror film with impossible special effects that defied the laws of physics and all human logic.

He had to reflect. To devise a plan. He turned on the ignition and drove off, heading down Ventana Boulevard until he eventually found himself speeding up Charlie Chaplin Boulevard, where he parked his car in front of the Nite Inn at Hollywood City. He'd stay the night there while he thought this through to the end.

14

He couldn't sleep Saturday night. His sheets were wet with perspiration, and he kicked off his bedclothes in exasperation.

Leo watched the sun rise through the motel room's sole window, and, dejected, he threw on his clothes and bolted out the door. He drove for an hour to the ocean, winding along the serpentine canyon road.

He pulled into the church's parking lot and took a moment to note its architecture, harkening back to the fifties in its functional simplicity. He was a few minutes late for 7:00 mass. It was Sunday, and most of the older parishioners had already found their spots in the pews. Leo caught the tail end of the Gospel reading as he entered through the front doors, passing the usher who gave him a paper copy of the day's liturgy.

Father Tom finished the reading with the appropriate closing: "The gospel of our Lord Jesus Christ," and the congregation responded with a jubilant shout, fired cannonball-like over the pews: "Amen!"

Leo found a seat near the back of the church and watched Father Tom take three steps down from the altar and plant himself squarely in front of the faithful, precisely midway between the two rows of pews so as not to suggest preference for one side of the church over the other. The homily was brief, as Catholic Church homilies go.

"As many of you know, I love reading short stories," he began. "Andre Dubus and Raymond Carver are two of my favorite authors. And you all know, when you read literature, your mind gets accustomed to thinking in metaphors—for Jesus it was parables. Symbols … allegories … and before you know it, much of the world becomes filled with the metaphorical, everywhere you turn."

He turned suddenly, for dramatic effect, to look at an elderly male parishioner to his left. Some in the pews chuckled at his humor. He took a few steps forward down the aisle, moving subtly into the body of the congregation, becoming one with them.

"So when I think about a small detail of the world, a detail so small it is almost invisible to the naked eye, I think of its universal—cosmic!—implications. This one small detail I'm thinking of—its name is actually bigger than the thing itself—is the *Emmenanthe penduliflora* seed, producing something commonly known as the Whispering Bells, a plant with bell-shaped flowers.

The flowers dry to a cream color on the plant and make whispering sounds in the wind.

The members of the congregation listened dutifully, wondering, Where is this metaphor going?

"The Whispering Bells have a very interesting cycle. They're an annual: a plant that completes its life cycle, from germination to the production of seed, within one year, and then dies."

He was keenly aware that his homily was beginning to sound too didactic, so he brought in a touch of the theatrical.

"An 'annual' flowers in the spring. Its seeds' germination only occurs after wildfires; the intense heat bursts them open."

He made a bursting gesture with his fingers, placing his fingertips together in a bunch, then quickly opened his hands wide. He stopped briefly, smiling, enjoying the thought, making eye contact with many of the parishioners.

"Remember the fire of two thousand seven? The one that forced local residents to evacuate their homes early one Saturday morning? You may remember this harrowing time. A wildfire that scorched some two hundred fifty acres in the hills above our very own church. The seaside landscape, once blanketed with wildflowers, transformed—in a matter of hours!—into a charred wasteland. But, depsite the devastating destruction, this little seed, this little seedling, took root and blossomed."

He took a moment, again for dramatic effect, to scan the faces of the parishioners.

"Sometimes you and I must experience the flames of suffering, but we know that through these fires we emerge reborn. But—"

He let the weighty conjunction sit for a beat.

"Never, *ever* wish for the Cross. The Cross will come to us at some point in our lives, it always does: that is what it means to be human, alive in this world, and in this fact we can all reconcile ourselves."

A few of them chuckled nervously. The priest went on to share with them the love he has for God's creation. He spoke of stewardship of the planet, of respect for nature, for the power of faith. And when it was all over, he clasped his hands, bent his chin downward, turned slowly, and returned quietly to his chair near the altar. And, as he always did after the homily, he spent the next sixty seconds with his eyes clenched closed, deep in prayer. Nobody spoke. The church was silent, for a full minute, except for the faint sound of traffic on the distant coast highway—metallic buzzing machines traversing dry asphalt on a warm day.

Leo closed his eyes too. *Perhaps all of life is a metaphor,* he thought. *Maybe none of it is real. Maybe it's a dream. Maybe I'm dreaming that I'm dreaming and it's all a metaphor.*

Except when it is real.

15

His meeting with the dean of faculty, his subsequent firing from Lofton, and the police search for his whereabouts (he had become a "person of interest," according to local law enforcement) as he wandered aimlessly from motel to motel: all this left him treading water in a vast sea of indecision without a visible shoreline.

Without his students, without his beloved routine at school—the black coffee in the morning, the papers to read, the quizzes to craft, the lesson plans to invent, the roundtable discussions to lead, the lectures to deliver, the faculty meetings to endure—without the ebb and flow of school daily life, Leo found himself with a sudden thirst for gin, even though he wasn't a drinker. But he knew he must stay clear-headed and resisted the temptation to drink. He turned to spirituality for solace.

During this itinerant period, while he motel-hopped around Ventana County, keeping his wanderings as clandestine as he could, he nevertheless made it a habit to drop by the Reverend Gerbajs's rectory office after Sunday's 11 a.m. mass, usually armed with a new collection of poems or stories that he thought his book-loving friend might enjoy.

Father Tom would never betray him. What's more, Leo envied this priest—a life dedicated to providing for the spiritual needs of others, and to being a communicator, counselor, educator, and leader—while Gerbajs in turn envied the English teacher: a life devoted to helping young people write well, appreciate good books, and honor their own ideas. Both men were celibate—Leo by the school's arid romantic prospects; Father Tom by vocational obligation—observing perfect and perpetual continence for the sake of the Kingdom of Heaven.

Moreover, both men lived like monks, more or less isolated from the getting and spending mainstream of American life. For Swift, the Academy functioned—*used* to function—as a quasi-monastery, an isolated, secular "City upon a Hill"; Father Tom rarely left the confines of the rectory or the church, located on the remotest westerly edge of Los Angeles County.

Sometimes the priest was too busy with parish business to chat with Leo, or sometimes he would have an appointment with another parishioner. Sometimes he was away, attending a conference or leading a retreat, for example, or simply indulging himself in a hike in the hills. But one Sunday afternoon, after three masses and a brief meeting with the parish accountant, whose unexpected visit further encumbered his myriad responsibilities—among his other roles he served as custodian, chief administrator, and general manager of all things relating to Most Pure Heart of Mary—Father Tom conferred with Leo in the rectory office. The space was magnificently lined with paperbacks and hardcovers from floor to ceiling on three walls—he was a voracious reader—leaving the fourth richly decorated with framed works of Native American art.

Father Tom established their routine. He would make a pot of coffee before they began their discussions. They met daily, usually after 7:00 morning chapel, in secret; Father Tom had instructed church staff to remain discreet regarding Leo's presence in the rectory. Like many ancient peoples, Father Tom recognized a religious right of asylum, protecting criminals (although Leo still hadn't been charged with anything) and exiles from legal action. "This principle was adopted by the early Christian church," he explained to Leo, "so you're safe here."

Their meetings addressed the requirements of the Rite of Christian Initiation of Adults, through which Leo would be allowed to participate in the Sacrament of Confirmation—and then, God willing, at Easter: Holy Communion. During these encounters, Father Tom would teach mostly by Socratic questioning. But eventually, after an hour of catechesis and spiritual ponderings, the exchange shifted to simple conversation, and they discussed such topics as literature, good wine, sometimes politics, and even their past lives.

During one of these encounters the bookish priest told Leo a story from his college days, because all notions of priestly formality, of the relationship of catechist to catechumen, had crumbled under the weight of friendship.

And wasn't friendship its own miracle?

16

During November 1964, around the time Mario Savio made his famous "put your bodies upon the gears" address as he led his fellow protesters into a sit-in at UC Berkeley's Sproul Hall, young Thomas Gerbajs fell in love with his T.A. Her name was Margery Grendalais. She was twenty-four and working on her master's degree, specializing in the late Romantics: Byron, Shelley, and Keats. Tom was twenty and landed in her English 117B class, a one-semester course that fulfilled an English major requirement. She was a few years older than Tom, but a spasm of recognition instantly rippled between them, as if they were twins separated at birth.

It was eerie, the quickness and potential combustibility of this attraction. It took only seven class meetings before one of them took action and only a month before the whole thing ignited like a Roman candle and then flamed out.

As he was leaving class, after she'd finished leading a discussion on the subject of doppelgängers in Poe's and Twain's stories, he slipped her a tiny folded note about the size of a postage stamp—placing it in the cup of her open palm as she shook his extended hand. She had no idea why he'd want to engage in this odd formality, this secret handshake; it was the sixties, after all, and most people abhorred any customs embraced by the older generation, preferring to flash the peace sign as a signal of friendship. Furthermore, she was a rebel, a fan of the atheistic poet Percy Bysshe Shelley and his equally defiant and brilliant wife Mary—and as she read the note, she smiled.

In minuscule, smudged, nearly hieroglyphic squiggles he'd written down his phone number. It took her a full two weeks, though, before she finally dialed it.

17

After picking her up in his rusting 1959 Volkswagen Beetle for their first date, Tom drove south on Telegraph and then headed west on their way to the Bay Bridge, Eric Burden howling *House of the Rising Sun* on the car radio. They came to a stop light at the intersection of Ashby and Fulton, and waited, in silence, for the light to turn. Tom twisted around to face her and saw only the shape of her lovely mouth, especially the odd downturn at the corners which always made her appear in a perennial state of skepticism. He kissed her, suddenly—he had no time to think, as he acted purely on impulse, giving her no warning at all. There's certainly a scientific explanation for this behavior: studies in neuroscience, for example, suggest that sexual attraction involves chemicals in the brain, including testosterone, estrogen, dopamine, norepinephrine, serotonin, oxytocin, and vasopressin. That said, although I am a scientist, I'm inclined to believe it was an unrestrained and heartfelt act of love.

There was no seat belt to restrain him—this was the sixties, as I mentioned, before they were required by law—and their bodies came together in an awkward thump. The smell of her perfume, an unfamiliar smell, not something from nature, struck his nostrils with an unexpected pungency. Locks of her hair wafted across his left cheek like a soft breeze. He kissed her perhaps too aggressively, some may argue, although once he felt her welcoming response, the kiss gave way to tenderness, and the ardent quality of the embrace surprised them both. It was Tom's first kiss. He was a late bloomer when it came to romance and by nature shy to boot. And so the sensations that coursed through him seemed galactic in scale, as if the gray concrete and stucco of the world had dissipated and faded ethereally away, his thoughts succumbing to the warmth of her lips, the spring moonlight, and the shifting air currents that roiled over them.

It took four irate honks from the car horn behind them for Tom to awaken from his love-sick trance.

18

Tom wasn't particularly social to begin with, so he enjoyed spending his free time in Cal's Doe Library, where he could lose himself in the stacks or find himself a remote carrel in which to study. He'd decided to major in comparative literature, partly because Margery inspired him with her own passion for literature, and partly because he'd attended Professor Lowenberg's extraordinarily popular American lit survey lectures focusing on the nineteenth-century artists Hawthorne and Melville. Or maybe it was the Beat poets he'd discovered while attending Professor Brown's lectures, which tended to place a Freudian and often humorous slant on the readings. Perhaps it was his studies of Mallarmé and Gide in the French lit course conducted by the ethereally beautiful Monique Auberge. More likely, though, the conversion took place while reading James Joyce's *Dubliners* stories, which represented for Tom, who'd recently been dazzled by

Joyce's *Portrait of the Young Artist as a Young Man*, the zenith in both artistic craftsmanship and in its understanding of human nature.

But certainly Margery's obsession with Byron, "mad, bad, and dangerous to know," had its influence too, since she rarely went a day without quoting from the Cantos. After a month of dating and late-night kissing, Tom's bloodstream seemed to flow not with red corpuscles and serotonin, but with the language of poesy.

I suspect he was in love. But Tom could only diagnose the symptoms the way a layman, a non-scientist, would. It occurred to him when he left Margery's apartment after an evening study session (she often tutored him in his essay writing) and couldn't find where he'd parked his car. One time he got lost driving home from her place and ended up in North Oakland, near the MacArthur Freeway. Another day he couldn't concentrate in his otherwise breathtaking Milton class, even when the professor recited the text in a most eloquent British accent, unlike anything Tom had ever heard, the final battle involving the Son of God single-handedly defeating the entire legion of angelic rebels and banishing them from Heaven. He even forgot one day how to read Old English in the Chaucer 111 seminar—the words could've been Swahili. And even King Lear's bloody rants suddenly sounded whiny.

Tom came from a Catholic family, the oldest of

the brood, with nine brothers and sisters. He'd never fully escaped his family's values—they honored the Gospel, for instance, with its notions about love, sex, and marriage—so he never pushed the matter of sex with Margery. Furthermore, he had no experience with sexual intercourse, and the act—to be entirely honest, he admitted—intimidated him, since he knew, at least in his subconscious, that once he crossed that hallowed threshold of a woman's body, once he committed to a woman in mind, body, and spirit, there was no turning back. All this, in lieu of the fact that Margery confided in him, after having downed two glasses of Chardonnay a bit too quickly one night, that she'd slept with three other men. One of them was a full professor of classics at Berkeley, tenured, who, when former graduate student Jack Weinberg was arrested the previous October while sitting at a CORE table in Sproul Plaza, joined a handful of other protesters and stood on the roof of the police car in which Jack was detained. The vehicle remained there for 32 hours; so did the protesters. Margery, who had read Mao's *Little Red Book* in a course entitled 270D:001: *From Yao to Mao: 5000 Years of Chinese History*, was enamored with the professor's prodigious intellectual gifts, his passionate political convictions, his articulateness in explaining Plato's theories of love, and, no doubt at the heart of it, his familiarity with Tantric sex. He was still calling her. She wasn't sure if she was 100 percent over him.

Still, those midnight encounters at her apartment, in which they discussed, often heatedly, such matters as the presence of God in atheist Shelley's "Ode to the West Wind," sometimes led to impassioned gropings—the lyricism of the poet's language had that effect on the two of them. Words as aphrodisiac. And when kissing no longer felt satisfactory, Tom—completely out of character, it would seem—suddenly took her hand and pressed her clawing fingers to his swelling self, a Doric sturdiness, as it were, and she latched on and squeezed to acknowledge the need.

But she lay curled like a comma—paused, with a suggestion of more to come—still holding onto to him, a knowing, uncritical smile gracing her mien as she looked into his eyes, and then she recited from memory, wistfully, Byron's verses:

> *Titan! to whose immortal eyes*
> *The sufferings of mortality,*
> *Seen in their sad reality,*
> *Were not as things that gods despise;*
> *What was thy pity's recompense?*
> *A silent suffering, and intense;*
> *The rock, the vulture, and the chain,*
> *All that the proud can feel of pain,*
> *The agony they do not show,*
> *The suffocating sense of woe,*
> *Which speaks but in its loneliness,*

And then is jealous lest the sky
Should have a listener, nor will sigh
Until its voice is echoless.

He understood very little of what was going on, his brain scuttled by desire. He wasn't sure if she was mocking or consoling him, or even flattering him (a *Titan*, no less!).

Still, he felt honored somehow, vaguely. He made a quick mental note to explore the verse another time, but now he could only moan with pleasure.

Suddenly she pulled away and, seemingly distracted, stood up and looked back and forth about the room, as if she'd misplaced a shoe. Lost for a moment, confused. Then she reassembled her clothing, now in a jumble as were his nerves, and asked him to leave.

For Tom, her behavior remained a mystery for years. She didn't explain anything. Some women were like that, Tom suspected, although he had so little experience with them; only what he'd read in literature. They were mysterious while beguiling, utterly desirable while elusive. He felt like Odysseus in thrall of Calypso. Jake Barnes impotently yearning for Lady Brett. Why would she even consider returning to the classics professor? Why did he still have a hold on her? After all, Tom had shared everything with her: his thoughts, his vision of the future, his painful desire for her. Why would she want anything else in life but to welcome him into her arms, to invite him into the warm depths of her body, to embrace what Fitzgerald called the "orgastic future" that he offered? He couldn't imagine that she felt differently.

But one Sunday morning the pygmy cypress outside his Blake Street house, which he shared with two other Cal students—a chemistry major who made LSD in the university lab, and a computer science major who'd written a paper recently on the future of America as a cashless society—smelled differently somehow, Tom thought. During the past two years, Tom had never noticed a smell at all emanating from this tree, but this day it smelled of lavender. Moreover, the sky had an unusual tint to it, cloudy blue, the color of faded jeans, not the seasonal vibrant azure sky cleaned by breezes sweeping under the Golden Gate and rushing eastward.

Sensing a change of seasons in the smell of the salt air wafting off the Bay and in the shifting light patterns caused by now thickening cloud cover, and feeling especially in love with Margery that morning, Tom decided to call Margery and ask her over for dinner.

She arrived a few minutes early. Tom had already spent all the money left in his savings account for that month on steaks and champagne from the local Park and Shop. He'd carefully set the stage in the dining room (his roommates obligingly left the house for the evening) by placing lit candles in strategic areas of the space, which created just the right ambience, he thought. He'd enhanced the dining room experience with every romantic nuance he could think of, including the music, which would be the Vogues' "You're the One," then followed perhaps by the Beatles, and maybe Martha and the Vandellas. After all, his guest was a romantic, a scholar with a taste for Byron, whose goatish appetite for women was well documented, a man who'd famously slept with two hundred women in his Venetian palace over the course of a single year.

Things didn't go according to script, however. She arrived a few minutes early, thereby blowing his timing. *A good sign*, he thought. *She's excited to be here.* But when he opened the door and found Margery standing outside in the moonlight, dressed in bell-bottom jeans and a top that bared her midriff—he remembers those details with perfect clarity—she took a quick look around. As she saw the candles and the bottle of champagne wedged in an ice bucket and heard Bob Dylan on the stereo upstairs ranting about how somebody would rather see him paralyzed—not quite the romantic touch he'd sought for her entrance; feeling the vibe emanating from this lovesick young man and knowing where this was leading to—Margery said abruptly: "I can't do this." She turned around and walked backed to her car, and then drove away into the night.

Overcome with a sense of failure, years away from being able to process his feelings appropriately, Tom recklessly pinched out the flames of his twenty-seven candles, singeing his fingertips. He grabbed his car keys and quickly climbed into his VW out front.

He drove across the Bay Bridge and sped through the city, getting off at Van Ness and following the glistening San Francisco waterfront, where he met up with Highway 101 again. As he crawled in his Beetle across the Golden Gate Bridge, he failed to notice the spectacular panoramic display: the City itself, off to the right, illuminated by a million tiny lights, glowing yellowish within a damp pillowcase of fog—he was lost in his thoughts. Margery's face haunted him, a face in the fog creeping along the City's hilly streets.

He drove north for an hour and a half and left the freeway in Petaluma. From Petaluma Boulevard he turned left onto Washington Street and drove on determined until Washington became Bodega Avenue. Several miles later he turned onto Highway 1.

He passed the post office on the corner and spotted a wooden sign posted in the shrubbery:

WELCOME TO BODEGA BAY, CALIFORNIA

The drive from Berkeley to Bodega Bay had exhausted his fuel supply but, even if his car had a fuel gauge, he wouldn't have noticed. The VW sputtered, gasping as it consumed the last vapors of fuel, and came to an abrupt stop in a parking lot. The engine shuttered violently and then died.

Tom noted the overpowering briny smell that

floated in from the nearby bay, and he spotted a bar and grill tucked in a storm of knee-high weeds off the road. He opened the door and stepped out of the VW.

It was empty except for a shaggy sunburned man in his fifties behind the bar, who asked for Tom's ID. Looking it over carefully, he said, "Just turned twenty-one, I see."

It was true. Tom had utterly forgotten about this fact, which had been of less importance earlier in the evening than the Winning of Margery. He thought that she could have toasted him on his birthday—if she'd stayed. Instead, the bartender paid for the first beer and wished him a long life.

Several beers later, Tom teetered out the bar's front door and realized he couldn't drive, even if there was a gas station to be found.

He trudged across the sand dunes along the water's edge, melancholia and nausea competing for his attention. Not only had he failed to top off the tank before leaving Berkeley, he'd forgotten to bring a jacket with him. Temperatures dropped to the upper 30s this time of year, and he felt the breeze bite him to the marrow. The gray stretch of beach looked bleaker than a moonscape.

He sat down on the cold, crisp sand and let out a moan. But the unsympathetically sharp wind off the sea quickly brought back his senses, and he remembered that he would have to find shelter soon. Too drunk to go on, though, he got on his knees and began to scrape with his cupped hands a trench like a wound into the loose sand, gouging it over and over until he'd made a significant dent, deep enough for a body to lie down in.

Margery was his first true love. He would have done anything to make her love him. That was at least how he felt a few hours ago.

But now, after his long drive and several beers, Tom buried himself up to his neck in his sandy coffin and fell asleep. He woke several times in the night, teeth chattering, shivering violently. Although he'd piled sand over himself up to his neck, he was still painfully cold. What he wanted, now that he felt more alone in the world than ever before, so cold and so barren of spirit, was for the beach to swallow him up. And he half-hoped too that when he awakened the next day, bone-chilled and dampened by the sea's nightly precipitation, he'd be in Paradise.

19

The fall semester ended and winter came. Tom and Margery recalibrated their courses and steered their bows in opposite directions, preparing for new classes and new beginnings.

One night many months later, he got a call from her. He picked up the phone, recognized her voice instantly, and greeted her politely, albeit coldly, and she asked him if he'd like to get together at Caffé Med over a coffee. She wanted to talk. Maybe she'd even apologize.

"I still have some of your things here in my apartment," Margery said, a touch of hope in her voice. She'd decided to take a reasonable approach.

But bitterness prevailed. "What things?" he said curtly. The coldness of that night on the beach still had embalmed his heart.

"You left that album of pictures, the ones from when you were a kid in Glendora. And I have some of your poetry," she said, suddenly oddly cheerful. "Some of it's pretty good."

The only copies of his poetry: poems that were meant to win her heart but could never compete with Byron, Shelley, Keats, Yeats, Wordsworth—any decent poet, for that matter. In fact, they were pretty awful, he suspected; they were maudlin tidbits rapidly composed in a loopy delirium of lovesickness, made of equal parts rhyme, iambic pentameter, and vanity. Still, they were mostly sincere efforts—from the heart, he felt strongly. And so without Margery in his life, without her lending flesh to his tortured strings of bony syllables, the poems became anathema to him, reminders of a light long ago extinguished.

The photos, unfortunately, were irreplaceable, placed into his guardianship by his mother, who lent them to him until next Christmas when he'd come home for vacation. But nevertheless, in an act of revenge emanating from the shadiest of sources—hubris—he shouted into the mouthpiece, with all the cruelty he could muster: "Keep the pictures, Margery. Think of them as little reminders of my love for you. *That you pissed away!*"

There was a frightening silence at the other end. Then, she offered, "I'm sorry," in a little voice. "I don't know what to—"

"Go find your professor boyfriend. You can read him some Aristotle while he—" Tom caught himself before taking it too far, but she caught his drift.

"I'm sorry" was all she could say.

"Damn it, Margery!" he said. He hung up the phone—*banged it down*—not even waiting for a reply, he sadly recalled. He didn't recognize his own voice. It frightened him: not just the metallic, shrill jangle of a broken phone disintegrating in his hand, but the utter vulgarity of his language, alien to his disposition and his reverent Catholic upbringing, emerging from somewhere else.

That was the last time he spoke to her. *The devil of a way to end a relationship,* he figured. Graceless. Vindictive. Nasty.

It wasn't until midway into Tom's senior year that he heard news of Margery Grendalais's death. His roommate, the chemistry student, had read in the *Daily Cal* that the beautiful aspiring professor of Romanticism had passed away. They found her at the bottom of Golden Bear pool, one of the university's four swimming facilities. She'd used her professor's passkey to access the facility after hours. A maintenance person found her at 10:37 p.m., alone, her body languishing at the bottom of the pool. A telling detail, which appeared near the end of the article: her blood alcohol level was 0.15.

More than forty years later, even after hours of therapy, Father Tom still wasn't entirely convinced that his brutal treatment of her over the phone didn't play some part in what he suspected was her suicide.

He really didn't have any direct proof that their phone conversation led to her drinking. It was merely a feeling, and that was all. Rationally speaking, it might have been anything: a single episode of binge drinking. An *accident*, in a word. It may have had nothing to do with him whatsoever.

But then again, she might have drunk herself into oblivion to numb the pain of a broken heart.

But wasn't his own heart broken the evening of his twenty-first birthday? *Who hurt whom?* he asked himself, irrationally indignant, full of blistering ire. And isn't this an example of an overdeveloped ego to suppose that *he*—this insignificant undergraduate, who failed to write a decent poem or, worse, to consummate his love for this woman—mattered to her at all? They were together only a few weeks, after all. A mere sneeze in the ever-steady inhaling and exhaling of her life.

"I made a deal with God," Father Tom explained carefully to Leo, smiling with bemused self-awareness now, a bit rosy-cheeked as he poured Doctor Swift a second inch of Scotch. "Although when God makes a deal with Satan, things don't go so well for poor old Job."

"God makes deals?" asked Leo, raising his eyebrows.

"I made one with Him in my naïveté at the time—I was in my twenties, remember. I like to think he heard me." The priest returned to his deep leather chair across from his friend, with the bookcase behind him forming a solid wall of titles, both esoteric and fictive: book titles as diverse as Reverend Raymond Brown's *Death of the Messiah* and John Irving's *A Prayer for Owen Meany*, Aquinas's *Commentary on the Eight Books of Physics* and the Riverside complete Shakespeare. This literary backdrop gave a wonderful gloss to much of what he said—he was, if nothing else, well read—although the whiskey lent an air of brazenness to the proceedings.

"I asked God to bring Margery back to life. To raise her from the dead, you could say," Tom continued, jovially. He'd made peace with his own history. "Lazarus-like."

"What were you willing to do in exchange for this miracle?"

"Leave Berkeley and a future in academia. I entered the seminary."

Leo nodded in affirmation.

"I was one of ten children. Staunch mass-every-Sunday Catholics, my parents always hoped I'd go into the priesthood, since I babysat my younger siblings so well, I guess—I was the best candidate of the bunch for a life of celibacy and service to the poor, in body or in spirit. And I wanted to please my mom," he said wistfully, as if this were another confession of sorts. "But more importantly, I wanted Margery back." He thought a moment about this. "No. I'm not being entirely frank with you." He took an empowering sip from the whiskey and rolled it around carefully in his mouth before swallowing. His eyes suddenly shown more brightly. "Truth is, I wanted to put an end to my feelings of guilt."

Swift nodded. It was strange to hear such candor coming from a man who made his living hearing other people's confessions.

"And there's nothing worse than Jewish guilt except Catholic guilt."

"But ..." and here Leo hesitated, searching carefully for the appropriate language.

Father Tom went on: "Margery did not in fact return from the dead. No resurrections this time, I'm afraid. And by then, after a lengthy period of mourning, I made the decision. I enrolled in St. Joseph's Seminary and was ordained to the priesthood in nineteen sixty-nine. Same year as Woodstock," he noted, smiling, thrusting an index finger upward sagely. "As everyone else's hair grew longer, mine got shorter. As the sexual revolution erupted volcanically, I took a vow of celibacy."

That spring, after many such conversations with Father Tom, even after a few more confessions on both sides, and after many hours of dutiful catechesis, Leo appeared before the congregation on the third night of the Sacred Triduum, the period of three days that begins with the liturgy of Holy Thursday, in which Leo heard the story of the Last Supper and witnessed a reenactment of the washing of the feet; followed the next night by the Good Friday liturgy, which honors Jesus's crucifixion; and ends on Saturday evening, when the baptized are more perfectly bound to the Church, enriched with the strength of the Holy Spirit. The essential dramatic, spiritual element, however, is the anointing of the person being confirmed with chrism, an aromatic oil that has been consecrated by the bishop. Father Tom approached his friend, who faced the congregation with his back to the altar, and, while smearing the sacred chrism with his thumb onto Leopold Swift's forehead, he said, "Be sealed with the Gift of the Holy Spirit."

Leo responded with the only word that fit, a little word, an ancient word that astonishingly took him right back into the classroom and the popular book blessings that always inaugurated a new literary text, that launched the students on a new journey of the heart and of the mind, literary lessons that would—if all went well, if Leo delivered literature to his students as a good French waiter delivers *les plats principaux* to his patrons, careful never to spill anything or to alter the chef's presentation, an expert on ingredients and flavors, able to point out which spice gives the dish its zesty flavor—help his students become more thoughtful and mostly more compassionate people.

"Amen."

20

He awakened in the bed of a Days Inn in Camarillo, a small town up the coast from L.A., with a clear sense of his own destiny. Leo had been on the move since he left Lofton. Driving from place to place, motel to motel. This was now what he envisioned: a life to be improvised—a life lived on a whim.

Leopold Swift left the comfort of his uterine motel bedroom, dressed, opened the front door, and set his foot outside. Never to return to this motel or any motel again. He'd never see his apartment, Lofton, or Los Angeles again. He wasn't sure he'd ever return to civilization, unless it was in handcuffs.

21

In late July, Father Tom and Doctor Swift left the church, bound for the Sierras. July weather in Southern California is basically Mediterranean. At the Santa Monica coast, outside the rectory, where the two men loaded their backpacking gear into Tom's Nissan, the temperature was a delightful 75 °F, while in Burbank, approximately 10 miles inland, it was 90 °F.

Overall, L.A. enjoys an average temperature of 84°F. This should be an excellent time of year to make the trip, they figured. But during the third week of July, in the place where they were heading, weather sometimes undergoes violent mood swings. In the Humphreys Basin, it could be 74° and perfectly comfortable before noon, and by 1 p.m. a thunderstorm could slam the Basin with the force of a wrathful god.

After driving north along Interstate 5 and eventually connecting to the 395, a three-hour ordeal, their journey took them deeper into desert country, through Joshua

Tree National Park and the Owens Valley.

Father Tom did the driving, while Swift day-dreamed. The rounded contours of the Alabama Hills appeared in the distance. Up the road, Leo could just make out Mount Whitney, which towers 14,000 feet above sea level, and the highway itself is 1,500 feet above the floor of Owens Valley.

As they traveled deeper into the valley, the landscape shed its greenery and became a rainbow of burnt-orange and reds, weathered, metamorphosed volcanic rock that is 150 to 200 million years old—timeless, it always feels to me, prehistoric certainly, a wilderness stripped bare of pride or prejudice, romance or realism, loss or redemption, painted lavishly by a god bearing a heavily steeped artist's palette. Some of the rock exposed here is 82- to 85-million-year-old biotite monzogranite, which weathers into boulders shaped like potatoes, or— from some angles and depending on one's mood—like Gargantuan piles of excrement.

For Father Tom and Leo it was a long, hypnotically spellbinding drive: Dust churned up by tires on asphalt blanketing the air. The mountains, reddish apparitions. Rugged, boulder-speckled terrain that looked Martian. The only indications of human existence were the thin ribbon of the highway and the occasional SUV or pickup truck.

Father Tom drove on. A sunny beautiful day of blue sky and dusty landscape, heating up rapidly. The roaring wind from the open windows made it impossible to speak, so they were lost in thought for most of the way. Leo enjoyed the peacefulness and watched the panorama zip past.

He was safe for now, he figured. In this desolate, remote world, nobody would track him down.

Miles of asphalt had put unpleasant personal history far behind Leo: the suddenly aborted career at Lofton, his clumsily ended relationship with Janice, his role in the death of Frannie, the seemingly endless, lonely nights in the apartment … a series of failures—now put behind him. He went over it in his mind. His life had been ordered, he'd once believed. Nothing especially heroic or worth noting in history books, he conceded. He'd done some good work at the high school. He'd helped a few young minds grow a little bit.

Before any thoughts of rebirth, he would first have to trace the trajectory. How did this happen, that he would be banished so ignominiously from the community? Forsaken by the classrooms he so loved? As he thought about the last twenty years, he saw the images fading or disappearing altogether, like cellulose nitrate film from Hollywood's silent era decaying into sticky paste.

22

L eo Swift met Janice Blackstone in a coffee shop in San Francisco. Long before she embarked on a career in nursing, she waitressed in the Noe Valley Café. She was the sole server that shift, the only one working there except for the cook, who was also the owner. She moved swiftly from table to table, a hummingbird flitting from stamen to stamen, pollinating the sleepy folk with caffeine, topping off coffee cups for hours. Not a conventional beauty, Janice—a little snaggle-toothed, a body without any straight lines or sharp points, all O's and spheres, oddly severe Louise Brooks bangs and a bounteous smile. Taken as a whole, she was Leo's idea of a Madonna of the Rocks.

Janice adroitly placed steaming plates of scrambled eggs and ham, or cheeseburgers and fries, in front of the neighborhood regulars—a blend of mostly young, upwardly mobile gays and straights—who sat patiently, even gratefully, at the counter as their beloved waitress, like a guardian angel, protected them from the day's imminent challenges.

What immediately struck Leo, though, as he took a seat at the counter, were the discrepancies. He found himself in a charming but plain local café, a 50s-era greasy spoon replete with Formica countertop, torn plastic seats in the booths, and an oil-splattered grill with its sizzling burgers—and there *she* was: a smile that was so dazzling, so full of good will that it banished all traces of the dreary morning; sparkling green eyes, that seemed to instantaneously lock into his; and long, thick reddish-brown hair—genes of her Irish mother and her one-sixteenth Cherokee father—that was woven in French braids and pinned on top of her head like a bonnet, making her look like a princess from the Brothers Grimm. "Rapunzel," he christened her. She was the loveliest human being he'd ever seen, and he knew right away that he must rescue this princess from her ketchup-bespattered tower.

He wolfed down his cheeseburger and cautiously asked her if she had plans after work, unsure of her response since she knew nothing about him. Janice said she'd hoped to go to a movie—Werner Herzog's *Fitzcarraldo*, he remembered—playing at the Breakers Theatre, a small art movie house located near the beach in the Outer Sunset.

He met her at her place that night, at the second floor of a Victorian duplex on 24th Street, and they walked together down to the Church Street trolley.

The journey to the theater, and much of the movie as well, were lost in his memory. The movie tells the tale of an Irishman known as Fitzcarraldo, who must pull a steamship over a steep hill in Peru in order to access a rich rubber territory—an odd choice for a first date, perhaps. But once they made it back to her apartment, Janice and Leo, unlike the obsessed hero of the film, effortlessly achieved a summit in her bedroom that night. They talked about their favorite movies while swigging at a bottle of Brut, which he'd bought at a corner liquor store on their way home. And around 2:30 in the morning—or was it later? She doesn't remember the precise time now—they toasted the stars, and then later, the dawning sun. And during the long night, interrupted only by sweet kisses that began as tender questioning and progressed to gradual discovery, they shared their stories—of dreams fuzzily formed and dissolved, of romances kindled and aborted, of plans speculated and then reshuffled.

By the time they'd finished their breakfast of scrambled eggs (slightly burned; she remembers that detail) and toast (rye), they'd already decided it was cheaper to share an apartment than to live separately.

23

He never became the college professor he'd dreamt about—teaching at Brown perhaps, maybe even Stanford—but he secured the job at Lofton, certainly respectable and more fulfilling than he ever imagined. A degree in literature, he well knew, presents few options, but in the absence of any useful skills, such as the ability to fix a leaky faucet, he knew that an English degree always carries with it the suggestion of intellectual exclusivity—he would forever belong to an elite club with prestigious academics as members. William Hazlitt, Robert Penn Warren, Mikhail Bakhtin, Robert Graves, Claude Rawson—these were some of his heroes. And Janice, likewise ambitious, entered Mount Saint Maureen's School of Nursing, studied painstakingly, earned straight A's and garnered an R.N. degree, specializing in pediatrics, launching her on a life of caring for children. For Leo, literature had the power to overwhelm him with emotion and be transformative; for Janice, children were the face of God.

Leo adored Janice, and years later, after they'd moved to L.A., where Carney Sandoe & Associates found him a teaching position, he grew to love his work at Lofton as well. He didn't want to alter the symmetry of his life, which was well tuned and humming as smoothly as a Porsche 944. He had this wonderful woman whom he loved, a fulfilling career in academia, and those magnificent mountain trails—so what else was there?

Consequently, at least it seemed at the time, his life was safe and predictable. The way things were supposed to work, he would've married and had kids, sometime around age thirty. It was more out of a feeling of lassitude, as well as the growing awareness of grey streaks appearing almost overnight in his hair, that he cultivated inaction, like a cherished backyard vegetable garden. He dragged his feet through life. Or, to mix metaphors, if Swift could place his order now to the Goddess of Waitresses in the heavens, he would ask for a main course of fresh halibut flame-broiled with butter—his favorite—and a side dish of status quo.

24

Chandler, Janice and Leo's daughter, had recently turned twenty, and overnight she became deeply interested in her biological father, whom she had never met. It was odd behavior, as Chandler had not exhibited any interest in him at all until then. Was it the beginning of a new decade and saying goodbye to her teens?

Her mother, in a mad burst of indignation and moral principle, had kept her pregnancy from Leo. After all, he'd made it very clear that he unequivocally did not want to be a father. Janice heard him clearly. So be it. Wish granted. That's fine. But how would this effect an innocent child?

When little Chandler, who inherited her father's Eastern European features and Caucasian round face, as well as her mother's Irish eyes, lush Cherokee hair, and unwavering certainty, was old enough to ask her mother about her missing dad (was it kindergarten when she began questioning?—Janice isn't sure), she always received a stern look and a quick, staccato reply: "Your father died. Don't ask me again."

She was speaking euphemistically, of course. His death, or his "passing away," which side-stepped the more traumatizing word "died" and the more accurate "disappeared," might sound to a four-year-old like something in a magic act. Rather, Janice meant that he'd moved on to another life, somewhere the hell else. Not here, anyway, not in this household. But she deliberately left it ambiguous so that the naïve little girl Chandler would have to interpret and wonder, as Leo's students would have to interpret literature. Word choice, syntax, tone, imagery, symbolism.

As a preschooler, Chandler understood well that any talk of her father was forbidden. Teachers and friends also came to recognize that her father was out of the picture and that she should avoid scrupulously bringing him up for fear of reprisal. And then, later in middle school, she began to envy her friends, who had handsome, tall fathers with deep voices—comforting, reassuring voices that exuded strength, sounded kingly—and large welcoming arms that wrapped protectively around them like solid tree limbs.

Then came high school. Because so many of the other kids—victims of divorces, shifting cultural norms, and untimely deaths in the family—were either fatherless or motherless, or were under the care of gay or lesbian couples, Chandler felt more or less normal.

But then came the turbulence of the Limbo Years—eighteen to twenty—when Chandler at first lashed out at her mother, cursing her for burying her father, for never saying a kind word about him, for rendering him *persona non grata,* for attempting to erase her progenitor from her consciousness by destroying all photos and records of the man.

She abruptly moved out of their apartment in North Hollywood, drove to the Westside in her dented black '93 Infiniti M30, with its broken left rear window that wouldn't roll up, the shuddering, spastic transmission, the bald tires, and the 232,412 miles on the odometer. She'd decided to utterly abandon her previous life, strip away all the emblematic signs of childhood and adolescence as a snake slithers out of its skin, taking with her only the clothes she was wearing (a skull-printing, sleeveless black vest and black Levis, as her mother recalled) and a copy of the New Jerusalem Bible, stolen from her mom's bedside table, with her favorite page bookmarked and a passage highlighted in yellow marker: *Anyone who comes to me without hating father, mother, wife, children, brothers, sisters, yes and his own life too, cannot be my disciple.*

Because she lacked a source of income, and because she refused to take any money from her mother—the father-rejecting, lying witch—Chandler was forced to live out of her car for nearly a month.

She soon became amazingly skilled at finding

relatively safe streets to park on at night, not far from Ocean Avenue in Santa Monica and within walking distance of a Jack in the Box, where she'd take daily sink baths using dampened paper towels, and where she'd purchase a cheeseburger and fries, her only meal of the day, if the panhandling went well. Some days she didn't eat at all.

The greasy diet eventually took its toll on her complexion. Moreover, at night she looked insubstantial, pale, specter-like in the blue glow of the streetlights. In the daylight, after spending so much time in the sun at intersections sitting cross-legged with a cardboard sign propped in her lap scratched crudely with charcoal, she looked overcooked. Rather, she looked "possessed," witnesses later reported.

I may be down and out, she repeatedly told herself, a mantra, *but I am free of the cruelest, most evil woman in the world.*

Her butt ached from sitting on the cement island near the onramp at Lincoln Boulevard and Olympic with her back propped up so she looked like a capital letter L against a cement pole bearing a crosswalk sign with the little iconic walking man flashing encouragingly overhead. She felt tired and hot, and a little bit dizzy, but she kept her homemade sign, a slice of discarded cardboard with the words JESUS WAS HOMELESS 2 written in charcoal across it, wedged between her knees. Undaunted by her misery, she kept staring into the quickly averted eyes of the drivers whose cars passed by, as loud as 747s, never slowing down, never missing a beat in their overscheduled day to hand her a crumpled bill. Waiting for a handout seemed to last an eternity, although once or twice an hour somebody with a look of genuine pity rolled down his window as he slowed, reached out to her with a dollar bill, and flicked it hurriedly into the wind or waited anxiously for her to take the handoff—if she was especially lucky it would be a twenty, but this usually came from the driver of the junkiest Ford Fiesta in town *because he understood her better than the others,* such as the rich dude rocketing by in his Cadillac Escalade, wearing a determined gaze that focused laser-like on the road ahead, as if his peripheral vision no longer registered anything but a gray no-man's land—Chandler suddenly felt so tired she had to leave her spot.

The walk to Lincoln Park took nearly an hour—she *hobbled* rather than walked. And the fact that the park was situated nowhere near her car made little difference to her, because she was so exhausted and the thought of stretching out on the cool grass, of lying down on a sweet green blanket of lawn instead of sitting upright on the sidewalk or curling up scrunched in the backseat of her car was grandly appealing.

She located her corner of the park, a more or less private area couched between two palm trees and the western edge of the tennis courts, but as soon as she unfurled her aching body and tossed her Jesus sign onto the still-damp grass (the sprinklers had gone off, for some bizarre reason, at 3:00 in the afternoon), an old man sat down beside her. He reeked of urine and feces, and when Chandler looked over at the source of the pungent odor, she saw a grizzled black man, perhaps in his seventies, hard to say, homelessness rendered him ageless really—he could be forty-seven or a hundred—with a white puff of chin hair and clothes so weathered and torn they reminded Chandler of refuse she'd seen washed up on the morning beach, haphazardly stitched together by magic forces. The old man began to talk to an invisible spirit off to his left, but she couldn't quite make out the words—something about a car payment he'd missed—and then, unexpectedly, his anger flaring Roman candle-like, he screamed: "Motherfucker! Therefore will I also deal in fury: mine eye shall not spare, neither will I have pity; and though they cry in mine ears with a loud voice, yet I will not hear them!"—and he grew angrier as he thought about the implications of his own words. He was clutching a large garbage bag full of empty soda cans and beer bottles in his left hand. In his right hand he held a child's plastic football no bigger than an avocado, and he suddenly called out—perhaps to the spirit partner, now in the distance, perhaps to his invisible tormentor: "Screen pass!" Jumping to his feet, the old man tossed the ball in a perfect spiral and it arced through the air. But there was no observable person there to receive the pass, and so the toy hit the ground, bouncing end over end into the shrubbery by the drinking fountain.

When she returned to her car, cardboard sign under her arm, she discovered that a bird had entered through its broken window. Fluttering maddeningly, panicked, a nightingale, plain brown except for the reddish tail, buff to white below, he flitted from window to window trying to escape. ("I figured he flew in while I was gone and forgot how he got in there," Chandler later explained.) She opened both doors, hoping the little guy would fly away. She waved her cardboard sign too, like a fan, and shouted entreaties at the frightened *Muscicapidae*. From a distance, from the perspective of passersby who could not see the trapped bird, Chandler appeared mad—just another pathetic, schizophrenic homeless person. But then the bird flew out the passenger-side window and bee-lined it into the branches of the nearest curbside tree, where he chirped his indignation.

Chandler, her heart beating in sync with the rhythm of the songbird's agitated melody, one of the most beautiful sounds in all of nature, climbed into her home on wheels and curled up in the back seat. She soon fell asleep, grateful to be, as the transcendentalist Emerson might have viewed the situation, connected to the Over-Soul, and striving wholeheartedly to do her best at, as Thoreau saw it, "cultivating poverty." At least for now, while she still had a roof over her head.

25

After another night of sporadic fits of sleep interrupted by the disembodied voices of passersby outside her car most likely discussing her homelessness--another humiliation after a day punctuated by them—she awoke to find a young man sitting astride a Suzuki motorcycle parked in the space just in front. He was perhaps twenty-five years old and he wore a pair of stylish Ray-Bans. His blue-black collar-length hair, almost DC Comics–superhero black, and equally dark three-day beard, stood out in stark contrast to his flaxen skin. He had the joyful look of an Edmond Dantès, confined to a windowless prison for years but soon to become a count. The heavenly blue eyes were what caught her attention most—radiant, she thought. And then, there was that smile. He turned to her—and *laughed*, of all things, not rudely but joyfully. Without a splinter of meanness. Not mockingly, but *knowingly*. As if her condition, as pathetic as she certainly appeared—

her cheeks were sucked in from malnutrition and her unwashed hair was oily and flattened—had its ironic side. As if God had a sense of humor, and this young man was in on the joke.

Cool as Marlon Brando, his Ray-Bans reflecting the brightening sun, he dismounted the bike and stepped over the stream of gutter water that flowed down the street. He walked calmly over to her Infiniti's open window to peer in and get a closer look at the young woman sitting in the back seat, hugging her knees to her chest. She sported dark, bruise-like circles under her eyes that made her look like a defeated boxer, and—outrageously, she thought—he laughed again. I can't believe this! Is he mocking me? As he gawked at her, open-mouthed, in a state of wonder, she gradually stopped feeling threatened.

On the strength of his disarming smile, she smiled back.

He then said "Good morning" and introduced himself, his voice pleasantly lively: "My name's Paul. Paul LeMot. What's yours?"

She didn't reply right away. She hadn't yet settled on her new name, now that "Chandler" was demoted to a character from an old novel she'd read and discarded. The best she could do for now was tilt her head quizzically as she gazed at this man. She'd left home on impulse. Now she would follow her father's genetic calling and act precipitately once again—with the sound of her mother's reprimanding voice in her ears, and against her own better judgment.

26

Wilderness permits are required year-round for the following:

All overnight /multi-night trips in the Ansel Adams, John Muir, Hoover, or Golden Trout Wilderness.

All overnight /multi-night trips that start in Inyo National Forest and will travel in Yosemite, Sequoia or Kings Canyon Wilderness.

The White Mountain Ranger Station at 798 North Main Street in Bishop posted several signs like this: helpful suggestions for hikers and backpackers. Admonitions, thought Leo.

Father Tom walked straight to the ranger's desk to

pick up the permit, which he'd reserved days before. The rules were thorough and succinct, requiring backpackers to respect the integrity of the trails and campsites.

None of this much interested Leo, since Father Tom took care of everything. But what most worried him was this sign, in red ink and gigantic font:

WARNING!
Be Bear Aware. Increase in Bear Activity.

Bear activity has increased not only in campgrounds, but in areas that do not normally receive heavy bear use.

Two extremely dry winters have decreased the available natural food sources for bears so they are looking for other food sources. While hibernating, bears enter a state of reduced body temperature, pulse rate, and respiration that conserves energy, but their "sleep" is not a deep one. Black bears leave the den periodically and continue to try to find food through winter.

Permit Policy

Group leader must have the permit with them during the trip.

Group leader signing the permit is responsible for ensuring that everyone in the group follows all of the rules and regulations during the wilderness trip.

Developed campsites have food storage lockers and bear-proof trashcans. Never leave food unattended at your campsite.

For more information please contact the Forest Visitor Centers.

STORE YOUR FOOD AND TRASH PROPERLY!!!

"You can't count on food being safe if you hang it in a tree," Father Tom explained sagely, as they drove up the steep incline leading to the trailhead. "I found out the hard way. My seminary buddy Franz and I made the mistake the first time we went hiking. We lost our entire week's supply the first night up—this was thirty years ago, like it was yesterday—by suspending two--supposedly bullet-proof, mind you—bags of our food high between two lodgepoles—*bullet-proof*. Can you believe it? The bear found a way to pull it down, ripped the thing to shreds, almost like it was made of paper, ate everything. Trail mix, free-dried beef Stroganoff. Food for the entire trip. We ended up cutting it short and headed home."

"I saw you packed a bear barrel in your backpack," said Leo as they rose higher into the mountains, the smell of pine through the open window, the air still hot.

"The thing is, they work. I keep my socks and underwear in it to conserve space," he noted informatively.

Leo nodded. There was much to learn from his friend.

"And whatever you do, DON'T KEEP FOOD IN YOUR TENT, FOR HOLY JESUS' SAKE," he stated emphatically. "A bear's sense of smell is seven times greater than that of a bloodhound. He'll sniff your food right out and tear your tent to pieces."

Swift shuddered, wincing as he pictured the obliteration of his ultralight Terra Nova tent, good for keeping out the elements but not local predators.

"That includes candy. To suck on while on the trail," said Leo. "I figured it'd give me extra energy for the switchbacks."

"That's fine and dandy. A good idea, actually. Just don't forget and leave some in your pocket. If there's candy in the tent, a bear will sniff it out. Advil, Tums, meds. Anything with a candy coating."

It wasn't the bears Leo was worried about. Since

Lofton, he lived in a perpetual state of paranoia. Even at this altitude.

This far away from home.

27

Burdened with thirty-five-pound backpacks, each one stuffed with a week's worth of essentials for life in the wilderness. The must-haves for safety, survival, and basic comfort: map, compass, sun protection, sunglasses, jacket, hat, pants, shorts, underwear, socks, flashlight, extra batteries, first-aid supplies, matches, knife or multi-tool repair kits, stove, a week's supply of food, water bottles, water treatment system, bear barrel. They'd weighed every item carefully on a scale back at the rectory.

But this was for a week's stay. If they decided to stay longer, they'd either return to town and restock—or they'd live off the land.

The two men left the trailhead and entered the John Muir Wilderness—leaving behind not only the town of Bishop, which sits at an elevation of about 4,100 feet, dwarfed by peaks nearby that tower nearly 14,000 feet, but their past incarnations as well. The trail ascended tenderly enough, the two of them moving up the path like fingers up Gargantua's spine, along slopes dotted with meadowy patches, aspen groves, and stands of lodgepole pine. Father Tom and Doctor Swift were soon greeted by a carrousel of wild flowers between granite slabs—paintbrush, tiger lily, columbine, tiger lily and—Tom's favorite—penstemon.

After the trail crisscrossed the Bishop Creek's north fork, the ascent became tougher. As they climbed their way through the pines, every step of their boots left a scar in the dirt. Their packs weighed heavily down on their hips, reminding Leo that gravity requires conscious negotiation, so that with each upward tilt of the trail, the body must compensate. A miscalculation and the pack could drag you keeling over backward.

"Up, up, one foot in front of the other!" commanded Father Tom.

They left quaking aspen behind, and the lodgepole became sparse. Limber pine, the nubbier stuff, sprung into view. Father Tom stopped to rest, contorting his upper torso as he twisted out of his pack, which clung stubbornly like a giant, piggybacking aphid. An amateur geologist, self-taught after years of trekking the Sierras, he sipped from the water tube that curved out of his pack and into his puckered mouth like a plastic proboscis, then pointed and swept his hand in a waving gesture over the panoramic view—a glaciated canyon floored with smooth granite and small alpine meadows.

"What you're looking at is the result of a glacier plowing right through," he explained. Their roles were shifting: priest was becoming teacher and the Sierras were his classroom. He stood more erect by the moment, his awareness of his pack's weight now erased by the joy of educating. "The Palisade Glacier has a history of thousands of years of glaciation. But what's happening here, the ecosystem is rapidly warming, so we're having more winter rains instead of snow." His demeanor shifted ever so slightly—Leo caught a glimpse—from the openly joyful towards the somber and reflective. "They're experiencing an earlier snowmelt with less snowpack. Disastrous for the critters! Many of the Sierra Nevada's native species have declined or disappeared altogether, I kid you not," he said sadly. He went on, now in full lecture mode. "There are approximately 570 vertebrate wildlife species that inhabit the Sierra Nevada region," he said, casually spouting facts like a professional naturalist. Clearly, he'd done his home-work. "Including 290 birds, 135 mammals, 46 reptiles, 37 amphibians, and 60 fish." Impressive, for a non-scientist. What he didn't mention are the 80 birds, 40 mammals, 10 reptiles, 20 amphibians, and 30 fish included on California's Special Animals List.

The endangered species. The ones that interest my hus-band and me.

Sitting together under a solitary pine with its tiny morsel of shade, Tom and Leo rested. Leo loved listening to Father Tom's fact-rich lectures on the indigenous flora and fauna, which he knew a great deal about, and on geology, a subject which he knew even better. Professor Swift enjoyed being Student Leo. He discovered that he actually preferred his new role, now that he was no longer teaching. A fine respite from his duties at Lofton. How faint in his memory the school seemed! And how blithely he climbed the trails now as his friend and mentor calmly took control of the entire expedition, leading the way on the trails, deciding when and where to rest, pointing out the exquisite intricacies of the penstemon, beloved by Native Americans for their medicinal properties, and all the other wonders of God's creation. When Father Tom gave one of his lectures, Leo listened attentively, very much enjoying his role as Alcibiades to Father Tom's Socrates. It was at the Battle of Potidaea in 432 BC that Socrates was said to have saved young Alcibiades' life.

During these moments of spiritual reflection, while sitting in the shade and catching their breaths, Leo had the first of many epiphanies on this trip. Father Tom made him feel safe. And the last time he felt this way was when his own father checked on him, a five-year-old, after he went to bed. In a nightly ritual, the little boy pretended to be asleep, but he felt his dad's presence in the doorway of his bedroom in their old house in Glendora, and smelled the faint male odors of sweat, cigar and gin: not terribly unpleasant fragrances at all, for they were his father's smells. Good smells triggering good associations. Peering into the dark with loving eyes, his father would scan the pile of blankets that defined the width and breath of his son. Years later, a cirrhosis-diseased liver ejected his father's soul from his body, sent it aloft into the heavens like a wisp of smoke, and Mom moved the dwindling family to a cheaper place in Van Nuys.

"I never got to tell my dad goodbye. He died during the night, in a nursing home, while I was still living at home. I never got to tell him how much I loved him." Leo—his beloved father's runaway offspring—looked over at his friend a bit sheepishly, suddenly aware that he'd forced Father back into the confessional.

After a period of reflective silence, Father Tom finally spoke: "You're telling him now," he said simply, his smile wide.

28

They each took a couple of swigs of water from their bottles and began the slow, painful ritual of struggling into their backpacks, twisting like Houdini as they worked the straps over their shoulders. As they forged ahead, the trail was flanked by the slab-topped, rusty cliffs of the Piute Crags, nearly thirteen thousand feet high, to the south, and Mount Emerson to the north.

Father Tom's hero, John Muir, had named the peak for his friend Ralph Waldo Emerson. They marveled at how the colossal granite slabs maintained their precarious perches, like toy tops belonging to a giant race of children.

"They all topple down eventually," explained Father Tom didactically and with great seriousness, as if the forces of nature were matters of life and death, which they often are. "The action of frost wedging. Adds to the piles of talus at the foot of the peak."

They entered the high country above Loch Leven,

where the glaciated canyon is floored with smooth granite and alpine meadows. A yellow-bellied marmot lay sunning itself on the dusty rocks, unmoved, either asleep or oddly fearless, and Tom, smiling, immediately thought of the beach back home and the bikinied starlets, a species indigenous to the Southland, sunning themselves on the hot sand without a care in the world. A few less brazen marmots dashed into the shadows.

For most of the hike up the pass, they followed a swishing, soothing creek. They encountered two easy crossings over the creek—man-made log bridges, decaying and splintery, some dating back to the FDR years of the Civilian Conservation Corps. Further up, they found a waterfall, with jutting boulders that acted like a funnel for the falls and reminded Leo of a snorting horse's head.

Soon, Tom and Leo were obliged to negotiate the toughest stretch, grueling switchbacks over the Piute Pass, 11,423 feet above sea level, and at long last, just as exhaustion seized them and began its throbbing grip on their calves and on their parched throats, the trail crested and then dropped in a jagged line into the magnificent Humphreys Basin, unexpectedly enormous and specked with high alpine lakes, cobalt blue in their heavenly clarity.

The view held Leo's gaze, and he spoke as if in a trance: "Far, far above, piercing the infinite sky, Mont Blanc appears —still, snowy, and serene;/ Its subject mountains their unearthly forms/Pile around it, ice and rock; broad vales between/Of frozen floods, unfathomable deeps,/Blue as the overhanging heaven, that spread/ And wind among the accumulated steeps;/A desert peopled by the storms alone."

Father Tom took a long look at his friend. "Wordsworth?" he ventured.

"No. Another Romantic. Percy Bysshe Shelley," said Leo. "Sublime, wouldn't you say? And what's more, not a soul in sight."

"Yes," said Father Tom, his gaze turning back to take in the spectacle. "That's the idea."

29

They set up a base camp one hundred feet from the edge of Desolation Lake. It is a place rarely visited by the amateur camper. It entices the occasional serious backpacker, or naturalists like myself. It also attracts the isolation-seeking misanthropes and misfits out there.

Father Tom began the ritual of erecting his tent. The surrounding landscape, with its stark batholithic granite foundation, suggested a grim, foreboding extra-terrestrial world flanked on all sides by pockets of dirty snow and a handful of scraggly pines above.

Bleak as it most certainly was, Father Tom loved this place.

His friend was more dubious. "Good God," said Leo as he surveyed the campsite and environs—the most unwelcoming place he'd ever seen.

"Yes. That's why I like it. Yosemite is jammed with tourists, it's a nightmare," said Father Tom, detecting Leo's hesitancy. "Here, just us. Hopefully, anyway."

And he added cheerfully, "Anyway, I feel closer to God up here."

They situated their tents—strategically, as pretty much every activity was undertaken with forethought in this harsh world—against a wall of granite twenty feet high and thirty feet wide that blocked the omnipresent nagging wind.

Towering Mount Humphreys stood regally overhead, its serrated top like a crown, its magnificent stature both comforting in its protective girth and terrifying in its sublimity—the mountain had a bulky, swelling presence that felt like it could crush them at any moment. Just as impressive, Mount Emerson flanked them on the right, an equally humbling authority figure. Both mountains demanded Leo's and Tom's attention, and the two men stood silently staring up at the jagged peaks—a little bit fearful, greatly reverential—at mountains that looked that afternoon like curmudgeonly 40-million-year-old granite kings, mad as hell at their subjects and out for blood.

30

Chandler liked riding on the back of Paul's motor-cycle—it was thrilling and risky, he was awfully good-looking, and danger appealed to her at this point in her life. Life on the streets hardens one. And she'd entrusted her fate to God.

The very first thing Paul said to her as she climbed onboard was, "She's a Suzuki GSX1250FA with a fuel-injected double overhead camshaft, twelve hundred ccs, four-valve, six speeds." Her eyes glazed over. None of this meant anything to Chandler, who preferred to know as little as necessary about machines or electronics, although she liked the way this man smiled with pride—a grin so charming and bright, so disarmingly genuine, emitting a warmth that touched off the dry kindling behind her ribcage—whenever he discussed matters regarding the bike, or, later in the relationship, regarding her.

But that day, in the late afternoon, she didn't like

feeling so exposed to the roaring wind, which buffeted her ears like a Florida hurricane, or the rush-hour traffic as he drove down Lincoln and then leaned the bike dangerously to one side as he navigated it onto the 10. As usual, traffic on the Santa Monica Freeway was at a near standstill, but Paul expertly weaved his bike between the cars, roaring and thundering, sometimes so close Chandler was sure her right arm grazed a few rear view mirrors. Simultaneously terrified and exhilarated, she fiercely clutched Paul's back, feeling like a baby monkey holding on to its mother as she swung through the upper branches. Her arms were wrapped like steel pinions round his waist.

She was keenly aware of the dangers she faced and the vulnerability she felt, aware that all it took was for one of these cars to suddenly swerve to the left and her life might come to a sudden horrific end. The odds, with all those cars and all those bad drivers, were terrible, she figured. She clearly visualized the worst happening, her body jettisoned from the back of the bike, struck by an oncoming car, and crushed beneath the wheels of another. What she feared most, though, if she were to fear anything at all, was hitting the concrete and sliding along the blacktop on her hands and torso—the way she remembered rocketing across the Slip 'n' Slide her mother laid out in the front yard—until her Skinny Levis were sheared off and her skin sliced away like a potato peel.

Chandler Blackstone had always had an "overactive imagination," or so her mother often told her. She was never quite sure what that meant. But what she completely failed to imagine this time was what, exactly, she'd do and say once she arrived at Paul's apartment in Royal Oaks.

Now hitting seventy, straddling the double-yellow line suturing the carpool lane to Lane #1, her hair lashing violently about her face as this stranger about whom she knew nothing commandeered the 405 freeway as it buckled over the Sepulveda Pass, Chandler suddenly became acutely aware of an inner peace that melted and then glowed around her like butter exposed to the sun.

Nothing to fear at all. The Holy Spirit would guide her and protect her, no matter what.

31

Both Father Tom and Doctor Swift packed lightweight tents, just big enough for each of them to lie prone in. Tom splurged this year and bought a MSR Hubba NX tent. Its unique pole configuration maximized his headroom and body space throughout the tent, which was important, for he was a big man and utilized every inch of space. Setting it up was easy enough with its color-coded hub-and-pole system, and the ultra-compact compression sack fit easily into his backpack. But what he really liked about it was its minimal weight: tent, rainfly and poles only came in at just two and a half pounds—the lightest tent he'd ever owned. Leo brought along his less fancy and heavier REI Co-op, the cheapest tent they had.

They had both tents up and secured against the evening winds, with heavy stones placed as anchors at the stakes, in half an hour. They moved stones, placed the stove and laid out utensils atop a flat rock that served as a table, propped up backpacks against a nearby tree, moved sleeping bags into tents.

It was home.

32

Her armpits were rank after three months, three weeks, and three days of sporadic sink baths in the closest Jack in the Box women's room; Paul assumed it would cause her embarrassment to reenter the world in this state. For his part, he had no problem with it and didn't notice or at least pretended not to; he was so enamored with her soulful eyes and her trusting smile that everything about her seemed lovely, pure, and perfect.

So he took her to his Royal Oaks apartment where she could clean up. His place was brightly lit with plenty of windows, furnished with colorful Ikea furniture, and tidy, with a faint rancid smell she couldn't immediately identify, although she discovered much later what it was: he hadn't run the garbage disposal in a while. Before she could catch herself, she imagined how she'd rearrange the couch and the stuffed chair in the living room so that the space would feel more enclosed, cozier.

There was a view from the upstairs bedroom facing Ventana Boulevard and the corner 76 station.

And although the furniture looked worn, a bit frayed and scruffy, tired like a beloved old pet terrier, the place was nevertheless clean with a masculine aura emanating brightly from the unexplored corners of the apartment—perhaps she caught a sour whiff of unwashed socks. Even the sink was free of dirty dishes, which surprised her for some reason. Chandler immediately felt comfortable.

He ran the water in the upstairs bathtub for her while she sipped from a cup of organic chamomile tea that he'd made for her the instant she entered the kitchen. They didn't say much to each other while he went about making her feel at home, or at least she doesn't remember anything now—perhaps she asked a polite question or two about how long he'd lived there, or he mentioned something about the thermostat or the cupboard door that always sticks. What she remembers most, though, was his congeniality, that devastatingly welcoming smile, his sweet and tender concern for her well-being. She remembers the hot bath, with its rising steam and its clean water, into which she settled herself once he'd left the bedroom to venture into the office down the hall where he would reread the screenplay he'd finished typing on his MacBook—his fifth feature script that year—that morning at the Cultured Coffee House.

Chandler luxuriated up to her neck in the healing water, cloudy now with the bath salts he'd offered her before leaving the bathroom. She liked the smell of the fumes wafting off the surface—they made her think of the Dead Sea, and then of the scrolls, and then of the ancient Jewish sect called the Essenes, which then led her to think about her confirmation classes at church—her mind romped about playfully, jumping from one thought to the next in the warm splendor of that bathtub.

When she stepped out of the tub, she felt a little giddy from the heat of the water, from the newness of her surroundings—from the changes within. She decided, spontaneously, that her new name would be Meadow. Meadow Nightingale. She'd rechristened herself, right then and there.

He'd also left a bathrobe for her next to the sink; it was several sizes too large and draped about her like something a Brobdingnagian might have worn. (After all, she is 5'2" and he is 6'4".) She found him in his office typing away on the desktop computer, focused and intense until she entered the room. He looked over at her and smiled.

"You must be tired."

"A little. The bath was wonderful," she said, closing her eyes as if to recall the feeling, then opening them. "Thanks."

"You're welcome."

He stared at her, wrapped in the white bathrobe.

"You look like at angel."

"I'm not an angel. I'm not sure what I am. Am I even human?" she said only half joking.

Warm tears began to stream one by one down her cheeks.

"You can have the other bedroom," he offered, reaching out and kindly brushing her tears gently away with the tips of two fingers. "I rented a two-bedroom apartment figuring family might come to stay. Hasn't happened yet. I keep hoping." That disarming smile again. "Clean sheets and fresh towels in the bathroom," he added.

She said nothing, involuntarily taking a small step backward as she wiped away the rest of the tears from a cheek with the back of her hand. Cautiously, reading her countenance carefully, he approached her a second time. She didn't move, so he opened his arms wide until he could feel her breath quickening and smell her shampooed hair.

As he embraced her, he asked, "Who are you?"

Chandler looked up but didn't attempt to answer.

33

That night she slept in a guest bedroom, and the sheets were cool, crisp and clean—until sometime in the late night or so, when she awoke with a start. She felt wildly disoriented; the room was shrouded in darkness, the bed a stranger's. Still wearing the bathrobe, she climbed out of bed and stumbled out of the room, catching a dresser with her elbow and crying out with a sharp "Ow!" as she walked into the unlit hallway. (She made a mental note to ask him for a night light for the hall.) At last, she found the entrance to the master bedroom. Then she was in his room—a new, undiscovered continent—and she let fall the bathrobe that bunched into a thick cotton nest about her ankles. Then she was beside him under the covers, embracing his broad back with her arms, pressing her breasts against his flesh, feeling small and vulnerable next to his large frame, feeling his warmth.

He slowly twisted himself to face her, and even

though it was coal-mine dark in there, they could see each other's eyes.

"My name is … Meadow Nightingale," she whispered tentatively. It was the first time she'd uttered that name to anyone.

It was barely perceptible, but she saw it, even in the darkness: he winked at her. "Ah ha!" he said. Then he smiled that unique smile. "Are you by any chance related to Florence? The nurse?"

She stared and then met his grin with her own—who is this guy? She figured, it was time to rise out of the River Jordan, shake off the muddy droplets of regret, and begin her ministry.

34

Meadow awoke to the sound of a dumpster banging raucously against the top edge of a green SoCal Waste Management truck, which was making its morning rounds outside Paul's apartment building. She found herself tangled in the folds of sky-blue sheets and a stone-white comforter, which for a split second made her think she was dead and floating in a cloud. But then, during the moment when the cacophonous banging of metal against metal intersected with a recurring dream in which her father's visage floated midair surrounded by licking flames (she'd never actually seen a picture of her father, so she always envisaged Gandalf's bearded, friendly countenance hovering before her)—she panicked. Where was she? How did she get here? She realized she was safe in his bed, and a glowing feeling of joy returned.

Donning his bathrobe, which he'd draped over a nearby stuffed Ikea chair, she padded down the carpeted stairs leading to the living room, half expecting to find her mother waiting for her with a damning expression overlaying her usual stern face, but where she found Paul fully dressed (jeans and a T-shirt) sitting in a Strandmon wing chair (she recalls this particular detail because they later decided to keep the one chair and donate most of the rest of his Swedish collection to Goodwill), reading the news.

When he failed to look up from his iPad as she reached the bottom of the stairs; when she stared expectantly at him, arms hugging the robe protectively about her, and he continued reading the *L.A. Times* Opinion section on the screen without noticing her appearance—it was an article on the recent Writers Guild walkout that had glued him to the page—Meadow felt the inexorable twinge of a very old nerve from deep within. She'd felt wanted, felt like she belonged. They'd made love just hours ago, and the Opinion section seemed trivial. Humdrum normalcy. So it seemed, in that panicky moment. For a moment she felt forsaken.

Actually, Paul had fallen in love with this strange young woman without a real name or a past—whether this constituted wisdom or folly, it was too soon to tell. But before he'd even realized she'd come downstairs, before he could welcome her into his arms and offer her a cup of coffee, Meadow had dashed upstairs, dressed, returned, and shot out the front door like a cottontail rabbit fleeing the hawk dive-bombing earthward, cutting through the vapor above.

35

B eing in his company was both a joy and an education. That's how Leo perceived his life with Father
Tom.

That morning Doctor Swift and Father Tom under-
took their morning ablutions; they dressed in their tents
(no mean feat in the confined space: one could barely sit
upright inside these canvas caskets); they stirred up a
breakfast of hot oat meal and dried fruit and nuts, rich
organic coffee carefully brewed over a portable propane
stove; and they donned their daypacks for the day's trek.

Once on the trail, little was said. Each man quickly
drifted into a meditative state as he followed the narrow
path, one of many trails forged by either Piute Indians,
miners, the park service, or, in the case of the narrowest
paths, critters including black bear, American Pika,
Ground Squirrel, the Yellow-Bellied Marmot, and the
endangered Sierra Nevada Bighorn Sheep.

When a trail led up the mountain and seemed untenable, Father Tom reminded his friend good-naturedly: "Don't look up. Just put one foot in front of the other."

Leo followed his friend's lead, trusting in his thirty years of experience as a hiker in the Sierras. What impressed him most was not only his leader's confident stride forward, but the sturdiness of his calf muscles. Tom's legs carried the massive torso up the slopes seemingly effortlessly while Leo struggled, loping behind, sometimes in great discomfort, his thigh muscles sometimes screaming in protest, sharp spears of pain shooting up his limbs. But the serenity of his hiking partner combined with the quiet peacefulness and utter beauty of his surroundings helped mitigate the soreness. Moreover, after an hour or so of climbing, serotonin in the brain kicks in, and so a sense of euphoria soon enveloped Leo like a warm cocoon.

Tom stopped to examine a small clump of flowers along the train. He bent closely to study the intricate anatomy of the tiny growth—*Pedicularis groenlandica*. The two upper petals form a curved trunk, while two lower petals flare into ears with a red-purple streak. The leaves are fern-like and the 12-inch spikes are covered with white hairs. He shifted into his professorial mode and explained: "Look at this little beauty. Elephant's Head! See? Look closer. Each flower has a long, pointed beak which curves upward, resembling the trunk of an elephant," he stated in a manner that might feel like a pedagogical assault to some but to Leo sounded like

Puccini. "Beautiful as these little fellows are, ingestion is not recommended," he further noted sagely. "It's partially parasitic and poisonous."

Leo frowned. Getting sick in the wilderness could spell disaster for a hiker.

"On the other hand," Tom continued, unwavering in his instructive enthusiasm, "some modern herbalists use it as a mild sedative and muscle relaxant. It depends! You have rheumatism or urinary problems? This is your plant. And just think," he said, pausing for effect. The punch line was coming. "Ojibwa Indians considered it an aphrodisiac."

"Great. It'll either poison me or turn me on." *Father Tom: priest, historian, geologist, botanist, standup comedian,* he thought. *Most of all: beloved friend.*

After another hour of winding their way across rugged terrain, they hiked over to Forsaken Lake. Five miles from their campsite, Forsaken is at 11,500 feet, one of the Sierras' highest lakes covering about three acres. There were almost no mosquitoes, not at that altitude, and the two men found a welcoming shady spot nestled in the rocks just above the lake. They called it good and set up a temporary camp. They each found smooth, flat rocks on which to perch, and unzipped their daypacks, fishing out bags of trail mix and water bottles. In silence, the two men stared meditatively at the lake as they munched on almonds and raisins.

It was there, at Forsaken Lake, that Doctor Swift

told Father Tom his story, without reservations of any kind, fully trusting: about the trouble at Lofton—about being fired, the investigation, his homelessness. Father Tom listened carefully, frowning, nodding occasionally, never interrupting. When Leo finished, he turned to his friend with an agonizing, half-expectant look, but said nothing further.

After reflecting on Leo's story, a look of grave seriousness on his face, Father Tom spoke: "I understand you must be feeling a great deal of pain." He then smiled kindly and said with great warmth, "But I just want you to know. You're safe here, Leo. With me. With the marmots. With God."

Leo nodded. This was some degree of consolation. He scanned the barren terrain around the lake. Then he looked up, as if taking a reading on his location. Looking for the metaphorical North Star, since the real one was invisible in the bright sky. He had strayed from the path, his original purpose, whatever that might have been. And for decades, teaching had defined every aspect of his life. But now he felt that he had completely lost his bearings.

From now on he would be living life without a proper map.

And then, after several minutes of further contemplation, Father Tom turned to his friend. "I can never quite get over how pristine and blue these lakes are."

"Not much pollution up here, I guess," said Swift,

his gaze returning to the lake.

"It's about as pure as any water on earth at this altitude, which is why the Park Service asks that we camp at least a hundred feet from the lakes." Back to didactic mode. "Can't do much about animal waste, of course. But we have to remain vigilant when it comes to human contamination."

"I don't think I'll be swimming in this water. It's gotta be like ice."

"Well, it is. Its source is the Palisades Glacier, remember? Left over from the Ice Age, which lasted between one-point-eight million years ago and ten thousand years ago. It's *literally* ice water."

"Where did you learn these facts, Father Tom? Not at the seminary, I take it."

"I'm more of a naturalist at heart than a religious," Father Tom replied. "Anyway, I see God in all this spectacle." He smiled and shook his head as he became pensive. "You know something? I'm always amazed when people ask me how I know God exists. What proof do you have? they ask me. I get that a lot. And I ask them right back: How do you know that stone-age man existed? How do you know *Homo sapiens* inhabited Spain, for instance, forty thousand years ago? I tell them, take a look at the paintings found on walls and ceilings in the El Castillo cave in Spain. The prehistoric artists are dead and gone, but we see their art. There's your evidence, bygod! They've left evidence of their existence behind. We know how old the paintings are, and we know a lot about who painted them *even though we've never actually seen the creators.* Take the cave at Altamira, for example. Beautiful, detailed paintings of bison, horses, aurochs, and deer, tracings of human hands as well as abstract patterns. *Man as creator!"*

And then Father Tom stood up and spread his arms wide, turning slowly as he gazed in wonder at the landscape before them. He reminded Leo of Moses, about to part the Sea of Reeds. "From huge, barren Desolation Lake all the way to turquoise Packsaddle Lake. From the mighty glacier above down to the intricate beauty of the basin's forest—*all of this* surpasses any human design. I say, *this* is God's artwork. *This* is his *Mona Lisa*, his Sistine Chapel ceiling, only his canvas is an entire planet. We're standing in the midst of a vast, divine masterpiece." He winked at his friend. "Evidence enough for me."

He continued standing for a full minute, gazing admiringly at the sculpting, color, and brushstrokes of the panorama before him, and then suddenly—as if nudged by an invisible hand—Father Tom, in a blur of motion, as if in one continuous gesture, yanked his sweat-saturated and grimy t-shirt over his head, exposing his pale, fleshy torso; unstrapped his hiker's boots and chucked them into the rocks; peeled off his hiker's pants, equally dirtied by time spent in the wilderness; and shimmied out of his Fruit-of-the-Loom briefs—then dashed straight for the lake in childlike glee.

For a brief moment Leo watched the heavy-set older man, with his younger man's muscled legs and youthful spirit, naked as Adam before the fall, hobble on the sharp pebbles to the water's edge.

His nakedness was shocking for only a moment. Leo felt that this man was a close friend, and yet the utter incongruity of the unfamiliar body in the context of a platonic friendship laid bare the gulf yet remaining between the two men.

The jolt passed quickly, though, giving way to an awareness of the naturalness of the human body released into the wilderness. Father Tom made his way up to his knees in the azure ice water, screaming "Ahhhhhh!" in either pain or joy, it was hard to tell, and then Doctor Swift stripped off his clothes as well. He watched as his friend then formed a V with his arms extending out in front of him and plunge into the blueness, disappearing from view, and, in Whitmanesque abandon, rise again, nod to Leo, shout, laugh, and toss his hair, flinging water in every direction.

Leo, conscious of his own nakedness but inspired by Father Tom's joyful exuberance as well as the Holy Spirit, bounded across the sand, granulated by a million years of the erosive forces of wind and rain, and hip-hopped into the water, shouting in response to the unexpectedly biting chill. He dove in, abandoning all restraint, and found himself wrapped in shocking liquid vibrancy, every nerve in his body stinging in indignation.

Wash me thoroughly from my iniquity, and cleanse me from my sin! thought Leo.

But when he surfaced and looked over at his friend, treading water just a few yards away—with only his Saint Nicolaus-bearded, grinning face visible, floating on the water's surface—Leo realized that he'd never be the same person he was just moments before.

He fully understood that, having been born of water and of Spirit, he would now be able to enter into the Kingdom of God. What's more, he knew that he loved this man, this respected priest of the church, whose face was dripping wet and whose knowing smile said everything that was needed to be said.

It said simply, "All is well."

36

Paul jaunted down the street and found Meadow at the corner of Ventana and Clarkson, standing in front of an antique shop. Several shops line the street at this end of Royal Oaks; this is where you go in L.A. if you want a relic from the past, a glimpse into past cultures, their customs, tastes, etiquette.

Meadow was standing facing the shop, head crooked to the side, looking intently at a window display. An antique wooden-drawer Elgin watchmaker's cabinet and a 1930s Art Deco Hammond Gregory synchronous mantle clock took center stage. Her eyes darted side to side like a kitten eyeing a dangling, swinging piece of yarn, as she scrutinized these objects, hypnotized, apparently lost in a daydream—at least this is how it seemed to Paul. *Why a clock?*

When he moved beside her to join in this inspection of old things, she did not move or show any sign that she was aware of his presence. He felt, of course, given the weighty importance of the night before, crushed. This moment—as painful and suffocating as it felt—was when he realized that he would not be able to live without her.

"It's really something," he said tentatively, referring to the clock.

"The cabinet is fantastic. It's really beautiful. But who in the world buys wind-up clocks anymore?" she asked without taking her eyes off the old machine. "Don't most people use smartphones for the time?"

"People who are romantics, that's who. My guess anyway. People who are old-fashioned at heart. People who value beautiful things."

"It *is* beautiful," she said decisively.

"Then it's yours. The cabinet and the clock."

She slowly turned to face him, her right eyebrow slowly rising like the back of a threatened cat. "Why would you do that?"

"Who knows? Maybe I'm one of those romantics. I guess, the way I feel right now, I'd give you anything in the world you wanted, if I could afford it." Her eyebrow lifted another notch. "Even if I couldn't afford it," he continued, "I'd steal the money, hold up a bank or something, and buy it anyway." This he stated matter-of-factly, as if it were common knowledge.

"Please. You can't do that." The eyebrow began to settle into its rightful place over her eye that was now pooling with tears. She crooked her head again, the way it was when she was gazing in the antique store window. "Why are you being so nice?"

He looked up at the sky. Nothing per se, just staring at the bland Southern California ceiling that always remained gray blue, no matter what the season. He scrunched up his face like a little boy, deliberately exaggerating his perplexity, then returned his gaze to her and said, boyishly, "I dunno. I'm not really sure. I just want you to have what you want."

She laughed nervously, pursed her lips and nodded doubtfully. "But what would I do with a cabinet, even if you bought it for me? I live in my car, for godsake."

He was pensive, but then he suddenly brightened. He placed his hand on her right shoulder and said, "Wait here. Don't go away. Promise?"

She nodded uncertainly. He then turned and grabbed the door handle and pulled hard on it, dashed into the store, disappearing into the dark interior. With the bright sunshine reflecting off the windows, Meadow could not see any further inside than the window display, and so she lost sight of Paul for several minutes. While she waited—unsure of Paul's motives and actions—*he's not really buying them, is he?*—unsure of anything except her own narrowed breathing, her heart's rapid beating, and the roaring buzz of the heavy traffic on this busy boulevard—time seemed to stop. She realized that at this precise moment she had no clue whatsoever where fate would take her. The feeling was both exhilarating and terrifying, comforting and anxiety provoking. The last time she felt this white-knuckle thrill was when she mounted Paul's motorcycle for the first time and sped off into the 405 traffic.

Paul emerged from the store with a smile on his face. He looked to her like a little boy who'd just caught a frog and was clutching it proudly in his two hands. But what he held so tightly and reverentially in his palms, clasped together like hands in prayer—sacred proof of something—was a store receipt.

"What did you just do?" she asked in utter disbelief.

"I bought the cabinet," he said catching his breath. "A watchmaker's cabinet, late nineteenth century."

She stared at him in horror.

"I bought the clock to go with it," he added triumphantly.

"Wait. I told you," she said, two parts embarrassment and one part irritation in her voice and eyes. "You know I don't have a place to live."

Without missing a beat, laughing in that knowing way of his, as when she first met him and he looked in the window of her ridiculous car and at her beat-down self, he said, "You do now. I had them ship the cabinet and clock to my apartment. *Our* apartment." And then, just to make sure she understood and wasn't mishearing him, he leaned into her, looked her squarely in her glistening eyes, took her hand in his, and said, "It's your home now," and added uncertainly, "but only if you want to."

He felt good about saying this to Meadow, although he couldn't think of a satisfactorily rational explanation for his behavior.

37

He took her for breakfast at a local spot popular with Oaksters, as people in this neighborhood of the Valley liked to be called, a small café named Fraught With Eggs-iety. Paul joked to Meadow as they took a booth in the back where would-be artists, screenwriters, and directors, or young actors hoping for stardom like to spend their morning hours, unfurling their MacBooks and attempting to write the next *Godfather* script or *Gatsby* novel, left alone by the waiters as they sip the best cappuccinos in town. "They're hoping and *eggs*-shus to be discovered," he said, stressing the first syllable, as they scooted into the faux-leather booth seats.

"But how do they make a living?" asked Meadow.

"All sorts of ways. Night jobs like waitering and bartending. Driving taxis. Working part-time for producers and agents, doing secretarial work mostly. That kind of thing."

"And you? What about you?"

"I have two screenplays currently optioned. One at an independent company named Dangerous Films—a thriller—and a low-budget comedy I wrote for Jude Hopkiss. My day job is writing for Enterprise Animation a show called *Carl and the Courageous Cockroaches*."

"Isn't that a kids' cartoon?"

"A cartoon *ostensibly* for kids, but we writers aim the jokes like poison arrows straight at adults. We try to amuse ourselves as much as our audience when we write the stuff." He smiled and shrugged his shoulders. "Hey, they like my work. I have fun. And it's a living."

A waiter brought them their menus. Paul asked Meadow if she liked cappuccinos, and when she said yes, he ordered two Italian capps. The waiter left, and they studied their menus quietly. Paul was the first to break the silence.

"Order whatever you like."

"I'm not that hungry."

He eyed her suspiciously. "Meadow, when was the last time you had a good meal?"

She did not answer but kept studying the menu.

"Please. I want you to eat all you want."

The waiter returned to take their orders, and they decided to split the special omelet. It was something of a compromise, as Meadow would gladly have eaten the whole thing. It was all terribly humiliating.

"We'd also like the yoghurt with organic blueberries," Paul told the waiter. "The large size. And two butter croissants." He winked at her as the waiter took their menus.

Sipping her cappuccino—she'd forgotten just how good espresso tasted. *Tastes like earth and sky in a cup*, she thought. She ventured forth: "Like what kind of jokes for the adults?"

"We're masters of ambiguity and innuendo, I guess you could say—when we're at our best. Carl's parents—cockroaches, remember—suffer from the same deficiencies as most human grown-ups. Like their kids walking in on them unannounced at one in the morning with tummy aches, at the most inopportune moments—that kind of thing. Carl, a five-year-old in roach years, doesn't understand why he has to take a daily shower when he's just going to crawl around in human garbage all day. For his five-year-old's brain, it makes absolutely no sense. But mom delivers a lecture on hygiene, and family image, and civilization, finally resorting to a threat to take away his iPad if he doesn't hit the shower right now. Meanwhile, Dad envies another roach who has a longer antenna than he does, and begins to suffer from Antennae Dysfunction—droopy antennae—medical doctors call it A.D.—leading to marital problems. We have one episode in which Dad and Mom attend a meeting with a certified marriage counselor, who tells them to spend more quality time together, away from the kids. Eventually his flaccid antennae perk up and all goes well."

Meadow's eyebrow curls into a tipped comma. "You actually get paid to write this stuff?"

"Depends. I can submit fifty plot ideas at a time—I can write them in an hour. They're called loglines—and the producer might like one. Maybe none. If he sees something promising, he'll tell me to go to step outline, then treatment, then script. Each stage earns me a check. For a week's work, from concept to finish, I'm paid what I'd normally get in a month driving a truck, which is what I used to do. What I really love about it is I never have to leave my apartment. Scripts are sent in via the internet."

"You drove a truck? You seem highly educated—literate, well-spoken."

"I was a literature major in college. Milton, Chaucer, Shakespeare. I don't have the extraverted personality of a teacher, so that didn't happen, and you're on your own in a truck, which fits my personality. I'm not that sociable."

"Okay. I get that. But how did you get from truck driver to script writer? That seems like quite a leap."

He stirred the foam floating on his espresso with his spoon. "For two years I drove trucks across the country, back and forth. L.A. to Chicago, Boston to San Francisco. Maybe twice a month. I'd pull off the highway at rest stops, and then work on my screenplays. After I'd written three feature scripts that I thought were good enough, I sent them to literary agents in Beverly

Hills—fifty agencies, big ones and little ones, in one blanket submission blitz—and finally a minnow took the bait."

"A Hollywood agent got you a job?"

"It wasn't that easy. Or that quick," he said, shaking his head.

"What do you mean? How does it work?"

"Well, I ended up getting together with this one agent. After a few dates, she began submitting my work." He looked at Meadow tentatively, measuring her response in millimeters of scrutiny, gauging the angle of her eyebrow. "It took about a year."

"You slept with her to get your stuff read?" Meadow's face got hot as she stared at Paul.

"I'm not saying that I didn't care about her, and she certainly knew what she was doing. She was five years older than me, but—look, I'm not proud of everything I've done in my life." He pursed his lips and looked down at the brown coffee swirl pattern in the cappuccino foam.

"Neither am I," responded Meadow quickly.

There was a long silence as they both sipped their capps thoughtfully, avoiding eye contact.

"I was hungry a lot of the time," said Meadow finally. "And cold. A guy I met a while ago, a guy about my age, in Lincoln Park, said he'd buy me dinner if I'd share the back seat of my car with him."

Paul nodded but said nothing. He watched the

waiter maneuver with the smoothness of a salamander through the tables to take another customer's order.

"It was a turkey burger from What Dreams Are Made Of Burgers. With sweet potato fries. And the creamiest, best-tasting milkshake I've ever had. Easily two thousand calories. Maybe three. But I hadn't eaten in four days, so I figured, five or six hundred calories per day."

"I've eaten there," he said simply, devoid of all sarcasm. "I know what you mean. It's fantastic." He glanced at her thin arms surreptitiously and then looked down again at his capp. "You're too—" He caught himself.

"I'm too skinny. Actually, I look anorexic. I know," she said. "But it's not an eating disorder." She took a sip of the capp. "It's poverty."

Then the waiter brought them their food, and Paul smiled at her with sympathy, and she smiled back. Not just with her lips but with her blue eyes.

"There's something bothering me," said Paul, bisecting the omelet in front of him and transporting one half to her plate with knife and fork. "Why did you run away this morning?"

Her fork hovered over her plate as she considered where to plunge it first. "I've had a lot of problems with abandonment. When I saw you engrossed in your iPad, looking as if there were no changes made to the status quo—after I'd met this beautiful young man and we'd made love and everything had changed, at least for me—I felt … I don't know. Unimportant, I guess is the word."

"I'm so sorry. I didn't realize--"

"A case of classic father abandonment, right? As old as history, I'm sure. Mom didn't care about me or my father." She stated these facts with cool dispassion. "I'm not very good with abandonment."

"That won't happen with me, Meadow. You're an angel dropped from the sky into my life."

"How can you say that? You just met me. You don't know me."

"Well, that's true. I guess there's no logical reason," he said. "But sometimes it's just a matter of faith, I guess."

She took a bite of egg topped with melted cheddar and avocado as she contemplated his explanation. She visibly shuddered. With joy.

"Oh, God …"

"Glad you like it," he beamed, looking at her eggs.

"No. What you said. Thank you, Paul," she said. "Thank you for your kindness."

He said nothing. Just kept smiling. She ate her breakfast ravenously.

"My real name is Chandler," she said between mouthfuls.

38

On their walk back to the apartment, Chandler explained to Paul why she had decided to leave home and live out of her car.

"I left in a hurry, for one thing. I don't have any money, and I didn't feel like imposing on any of my friends. Basically, I just wanted to drop off the planet until I figured out my next move. I wanted to be anonymous, without any ties to the human race, adrift—incognito, like a circus clown," she told Paul.

"But you must have suffered. Living on the streets must be hell."

"I guess I've been punishing myself."

"For what?"

"I'm not really sure. I've given it a lot of thought, though. For not feeling worthy of having a real father who really loves me enough to raise me. For having a mother who prevented me from knowing my father," she said.

"Where is your dad?"

"I have no idea. I've never met him."

"You don't know where he lives?" Paul asked. "Nothing? How is that possible?"

"I don't even know if he's alive," she said, unoffended by his challenge; she'd been asked this question many times. She turned to Paul, smiling. "I know I had a father for a brief moment, at least—that much I know about how babies are made."

"You think he was a sperm donor? Maybe your mom doesn't know the guy herself."

"No. Mom dropped a few inadvertent comments— remarks like little telltale rabbit pellets on the lawn— over the years. They lived together for years. She hates him."

"No records? Photo albums?"

"Not a thing. I mean, there probably were. She just threw everything out."

They came to the apartment and Paul dug into his pocket for the key. After letting them in, he turned to Chandler and placed his large hands gently on her shoulders.

"Chandler," he said evenly and as gently as he could, "how can you trust me, believe in *us,* if you have this *thing* weighing down on you?"

"What thing?"

"You're a wounded soul. You've been betrayed by your mother and father who have denied you the truth."

He caught himself and apologized. "I don't mean to stick my nose into your business."

"It's okay. I trust you," she replied. "I trust my intuition about things."

"Well, okay then." He crossed over to the table nearby where his laptop rested, and sat at the chair. Chandler stayed standing. "I think you're carrying too much pain inside. You can't go into a new relationship with such terribly important questions left unresolved."

"Probably so," she said. "What do you propose I do, Doctor Freud?"

"Do an internet search. Track the man down like a private investigator."

She smiled. "Sounds like one of your screenplays."

He opened the laptop and the screen lit up. He typed in a password, and a second or two later he was staring at the desktop: the image of a cartoon cockroach. Another click and Google filled the screen.

"What's your mom's name?" he asked.

"Janice Blackstone. I've always assumed it's her real name."

He looked back at her. "So your name's Chandler Blackstone? Good to know. I like it. Sounds like a name from a novel." He promptly typed in her mother's name in the search box, and in seconds there were 2,607 results. Chandler moved in behind him and leaned over his shoulder toward the screen. "Did you know if she has a Twitter account?"

"I don't know what she does with her time," she replied flatly.

"One website, called YourLife.com, says she lives in Van Nuys. She was born in 'sixty-two." He clicked the back button and scrolled down the page. He stopped and stared. "She ever work in the Peace Corps?"

"Not a chance. Wrong Blackstone. The proverbial needle in the haystack?"

"Maybe not that bad. With a little patience … Was she an investigative journalist?"

"Hardly."

"Wait. Here's something." He clicked twice and leaned in closer. "Another site that claims they have complete contact info for people you can't find any-where else."

And there it was. The site listed her mother's name, her own name, and a man's name: Doctor Leopold Swift, the only one associated with the mother, along with birth dates, places of birth, and current residences.

"It says your dad—I'm sure "Swift" is the guy we're looking for. Works at Lofton Academy. Did he change his name?"

Paul then typed in Doctor Swift's name in the search engine and clicked "GO." They both waited anxiously as a fresh page popped on the screen. The first listing appeared in blue against a white background:

Doctor Leopold Swift English teacher/ EvaluateMyTeacher.com
Doctor Leopold Swift/ LinkedIn
Doctor Leopold Swift/ZoomZoomInfo.com
Images of Doctor Leopold Swift

"What do you know. Your dad teaches English!" called out Paul, brightening. "We're kindred spirits."

Chandler stared at the series of tiny images of her father. He reminded her of an elf from Middle Earth. A benign, vaguely handsome face of a man in his late fifties, maybe early sixties. A sweet face, kindly looking, she felt. Although technically a stranger, he projected certain family characteristics which she'd seen in the mirror before: the nose, the eyes, even the smile—they were in her genes. She knew he was her father, and she knew that she would see him soon.

"Hey, look at this," said Paul. "There's an article here from the *L.A. Star News.*" He began reading to himself, suddenly looking grave. "Oh, crap ..."

"What?" Chandler asked, squeezing in next to Paul on the swivel chair. She began reading to herself. Her eyes went in and out of focus as blood pulsed hard in her veins.

The Los Angeles Police Department is investigating allegations that a teacher carried out an "inappropriate relationship" with a student at one of Los Angeles' most prestigious private schools ...

And farther down:

Allegations that former Lofton Academy English teacher Doctor Swift was involved with a student ...

And below that:

Lofton has recruited a member of its Board of Trustees, Myra Glick, to chair a special investigative committee, according to a statement from the school.

Paul turned to Chandler, whose face was inches away from his. She was still reading raptly.

"My God, Chandler, I –"

"Stop. I'm still reading," she said calmly as if she were reading the directions on the back of a medication bottle.

He waited, and then finally: "You okay?"

"I'm fine," she said, still reading, focused, unblinking.

The expression "Some stones are better left unturned" crossed Paul's mind and he almost said it out loud.

"You mind if I sit at your computer for a little bit?

I'd like to read everything there is on my dad," she said quietly.

Paul stood and Chandler, still highly focused, sat directly in front of the laptop, her gaze never veering from the screen.

"I'd like to find out all I can and then—" She looked up at Paul, who remained at her side. "Then I would like to visit the school where he taught. It's just a few miles from here."

"It's summer, Chandler. Probably no one's there."

"Not the students or teachers. But I'll bet some of the administrators work during the summer. Someone can help me."

"We can leave when you're finished."

She smiled faintly, torn between great anxiety over the news of her father and her gratitude for Paul's support, and returned her gaze to the glowing computer screen.

39

Lieutenant Maximiliano Alvarado of the L.A.P.D. had hard, inquisitive eyes that somehow simultaneously accused and exonerated you as he listened to your story. Under his gaze, you felt damned either way. He liked to dress fashionably in perfectly tailored Hugo Boss suits, and the effect of his well-tailored look was disarming. Clients trusted this dapper man. The cut of the suits successfully downplayed the middle-age paunch that rested on his loins like a bulging kangaroo pouch. His weaknesses were imported beer, especially Stella Artois, food from La Fortaleza in East Los Angeles, and Adobo, a ubiquitous dish in nearly every household in the Philippines. As romantic as detective work seems, the Lieutenant's job is mostly sedentary, which exacerbates his nearly hopeless weight problem.

Lieutenant Alvarado was a member of the Valley division of the Detective Support and Vice Division (DSVD), which is responsible for investigating missing persons, hate crimes, threats made to public officials and other prominent persons, aggravated stalking, piracy and counterfeit sales, animal cruelty, pimping, pandering, pornography, prostitution, and human trafficking. He rubs elbows daily with druggies, pimps, pushers, prostitutes, bootleggers, bookies, mob lords, thugs, and gangsters. He'd recently closed a particularly nasty case; it haunted his dreams for days. He'd led an investigation into the latest casualties in the dope scourge plaguing the Valley. He and his buddies found two dead junkies—a husband and wife, both jazz musicians—in a squalid apartment, surgical tubing still wrapped tightly around their track-pocked arms. Still hiding in a bedroom closet huddled their five-year-old daughter, a little girl named Monica, who had large eyes like one of those adorable children in a Margaret Keane painting. No matter how hard the lieutenant tried to scour the imagery from his mind with an imagined Brillo soap pad—by consuming sleeping pills, Coronas, or Prozac, whichever was closest at hand—the girl's face remained fixed on the inside wall of his skull, like one of the shadowy human outlines found on surfaces near the great blast at Nagasaki.

The Roman Catholic Church sees crime a bit differently than does the L.A.P.D. The Church thinks in terms of fallenness. It distinguishes between vice, which is a habit of sin, and the sin itself, which is an individual morally improper act. But Lieutenant Alvarado, who was born in Mexico, did not belong to the community of Catholics in the L.A. Archdiocese. Although the majority of the city's Catholic population is Hispanic, the lieutenant is that rare species: a Hispanic Buddhist who is also a vice cop. He'd been one since the sixties, when as a devoted Beatles fan, inspired by their interest in Hinduism and its music, he opened up to the teachings of Siddhartha Gautama, the Buddha. They led him to a religious conversion and he abandoned Catholicism forever.

His new religion shaped his thinking every day. But the foremost principle that governed his daily life was the avoidance of unwholesome actions and the cultivation of positive actions. In the Sarvastivadin tradition of Buddhism—the lieutenant's—there are 108 defilements—or vices—which are prohibited. These are subdivided into 10 bonds: absence of shame, absence of embarrassment, jealousy, parsimony, remorse, drowsiness, distraction, torpor, anger, and concealment of wrongdoing.

The lieutenant knew too well that he'd committed most of the Sarvastivadin defilements, sometimes more than one in a single day. It is for this reason that humility has always tempered his work. When arresting a citizen, it wasn't a sin he or she'd committed; rather, it was some city decree—simple as that.

There is a universal moral code and then there is

the Los Angeles penal code. The lieutenant kept the two opposing forces balanced in his mind like a child's teeter-totter.

He stared hungrily at his lunch. Hoping to mix it up, he'd ordered take-out from Wong's Wok Chinese Food around the corner. The three dishes—cream cheese wontons, house special chow mein, and orange peel chicken—were still in their cartons, and he arranged them in a triangular pattern, in the shape of an ancient pyramid, before him on his narrow desk. Chop sticks in hand, he closed his eyes and said, softly, so his colleagues in the office wouldn't overhear, a Buddhist meal gatha:

> We receive this food in gratitude to all beings
> Who have helped to bring it to our table,
> And vow to respond in turn to those in need
> With wisdom and compassion.

He needed fortifying, spiritually and physically, what with all manner of sin impinging on his day.

40

Lofton's headmaster wore large glasses with heavy black frames that rested on a stubby nose of a round face. He had a receding hairline, which made the top of his head as smooth as a freshly laid egg. Thick eyelids turned his stare into a squint. The headmaster reminded Paul of Humpty Dumpty: an anthropomorphic egg teetering on a squeaky swivel chair behind a formidable, hulking mahogany desk. Paul, who reflexively thought of the world in terms of endless animation series possibilities, quickly imagined the logline:

Elmore Egg tumbles off his perch during a Board of Trustees meeting, and all the board's lawyers and all the school's directors can't put Elmore together again. The students end up making a giant omelet of him and serving the headmaster for breakfast on Commencement Day.

The affable headmaster squinted at Paul and then Chandler. His stare made Chandler feel as if she and Paul, not of the Lofton community, were oddities in the Cabinet of Curiosities, an embryonic horse or a pygmy shrunken head or the Vegetable Lamb of Tartary or a miniature unicorn preserved in formaldehyde. Squirming under his relentless gaze, Chandler glanced at Paul hoping for help.

Thinking deeply about how he might write a new animation series starring this man, Paul could only offer her a subtle roll of the eyes and a faint smile for support.

The headmaster opened a desk drawer and reached inside. He felt around with his cucumber fingers and pulled out a small scrap of paper, crinkled and soiled, yellow-stained. He unfolded it carefully and, without looking at the words, scribbled, in miniscule, crimped pencil markings, looked pleadingly at Chandler. He suddenly appeared much older than his fifty-four years.

"You know, I always write down the name of a student who has passed away on this little scrap of paper," he said, pausing in respectful silence. "We've had four suicides, three sports-related deaths, two fatal car accidents—all in my relatively short tenure here at Lofton." He seemed sincerely crushed.

Chandler could only stare at the headmaster in disbelief. "That's so sad," she said, after a shocked pause.

"It is indeed." He suddenly looked weary, his face deflating with sadness. He carefully returned the grizzled paper fragment to its burrow in his desk. "We all loved Frannie Upstead," he continued, closing his eyes as if to recall her image, then opening them, looking around disconcertedly, as if the office were suddenly unfamiliar. Then focusing on Chandler at last, with squinting eyes: "We like to think of her as a Lofton treasure—now lost. The crown jewels of this academy are our students," he said now smiling. "People, you see, not awards or fame or even endowments, are our most important asset."

Something—was it years of administrative work in a distinguished private school that was forever in the public eye?—had turned him into a human platitude. Were his words heavily rehearsed? Spoken routinely, from rote, or from the heart?

Again, Chandler threw a glance at Paul seeking help. *What is he implying?* she wanted to ask him. In the short span of two days, since awakening to Paul mounted on his bike on a city side street, she'd come to think of him as her trusted confidant. *Is he accusing me of something? Where is this leading?* And again, Paul could only smile supportively.

"I had no idea your dad had a child," the head-master said, suddenly cheerful, as if the grim list of names and Frannie's ghostly face had dissipated like morning fog.

"I've never met my father," Chandler replied simply. She felt numb from repeating this fact to acquaintances and strangers alike over the course of her life, too many times. "I had no idea he was a teacher here until we did a Google search."

"How is that possible? He's been a teacher here for seventeen years."

"My mother never spoke of him. He didn't exist. Persona non grata."

"You weren't curious?"

"As far as I knew, he was dead. No, that's not it. He never existed."

Despite the fact that the headmaster had worked in high schools for thirty-two years, this was apparently a new twist. He blinked at her searchingly, his eyes emerging from the squint, now balled like little eggs. "Oh, my. Well, good things come to those who wait," he said encouragingly.

"I guess I felt this was the right time. Actually, I don't know why I came here."

"Time heals –"

"All wounds. I suppose so." She suddenly felt she'd made a terrible mistake. Her spine stiffened as she prepared to stand.

But then, almost as an afterthought, he continued: "Your dad is in a bit of trouble, Chandler." His tone was grave as he leaned back, placing his hands behind his head.

"Yes, I know. I've read the news online."

"It doesn't look good, I'm very sorry to say."

He returned his hands to his lap, leaned forward in his chair, and clasped his hands together, as if he were her confessor. "Why are you here, Chandler? What can I do for you?"

She closed her eyes, weighing her options. She then looked at him squarely. Here was a man who'd known her father for almost two decades, almost as long as she'd been alive.

"My dad was so busy living his life, being a teacher, being obsessed with other things. He didn't have time to be my father," she said without a trace of irony in her voice. "I'm not bitter. It's just the way it is." And then, after a moment of reflection: "My mom never talked about him, in fact she forbade any talk of him. But I always imagined he was a big baby—that's all."

The door suddenly opened. The headmaster abruptly stood to greet the intruder. "Detective Alvarado." He gestured to Chandler. "Detective, this is Chandler Blackstone, Doctor Swift's daughter." Nodding towards Paul: "And this is her friend, Paul—le Mat is it?" he asked, rhyming his last name with "gnat."

"Le *Mot*," said Paul, flinching.

"The word. Indeed," said the headmaster. Paul couldn't tell if he was being ironic, but he brushed it off.

The Detective reached into his coat pocket and flipped out a badge. "Lieutenant Maximiliano Alvarado, L.A.P.D., Valley division."

For a second Chandler could only stare, with a mixture of curiosity and alarm.

"I'd like to talk to you, if you don't mind," said the lieutenant benignly, his impeccable dress adding a layer of charm. Oddly, the eyes were both reproving and welcoming at once, thought Chandler. "It won't take long."

The Buddha says, "Life is suffering." This deceptively straightforward philosophical point reminds his followers that life is not ultimate and lasting, and hence we should strive towards Buddhahood—a permanent and perfect life. The lieutenant tried to remember this fundamental truth. He also tried to remember that it was his job, a duty, as he took a seat across from Chandler to begin his questioning.

For a moment Paul thought Chandler might lose her composure. Talking about her dad was clearly a source of great pain. But he was wrong. She answered the barrage of questions calmly, dispassionately. She didn't have any idea where her father was. She didn't think her mom had kept in touch.

The line of questioning went nowhere. She didn't, in fact, know anything about the man at all.

41

Perched on a rocky slope, the lake was visible from their campsite, through a clump of stunted pines. After returning from their day hike, Father Tom and Doctor Swift rested in their space-module tents. They were beat. But in an hour, after a short nap, while Doctor Swift still slept, Father Tom sprang from his tent with renewed vigor, as if the grueling hike back to their campsite and the arctic swim had never happened. He scooped out his fishing gear from his backpack: an Ultralight 8-inch Collapsible Fishing Pen Rod with a MINI reel. Without saying a word to his partner, quiet in the solemnity of the moment, for indeed fishing for one's meal is ancient as the evening breeze, Father Tom, a "fisher of men" as well as of golden trout, gathered up his gear and trekked down to the water's edge.

42

When Leo awoke he was disoriented at first. He had a searing oxygen-deprivation headache, resulting from the high altitude. He kept several individual packets of Advil by his "pillow"—a rolled up pair of jeans—for this purpose. The tent's green ceiling stretched in an arc only a foot above his face. He was lying rigidly on his back; the ground was hard and made reclining on his side too painful. The confined space exacerbated his discomfort. The snug walls, boxy interior, coffin-like. Still prone, Leo routed out the Advil and tore open the packet. He took the two tablets and washed them down with water from the bottle he kept by the screen door. The water was warm and tasted like plastic.

These brief catnaps in the afternoon always threw off Leo's sleep cycle and made him dizzy, but he'd been exhausted, conquered by Morpheus, the winged daemon who mimicked a Steller's jay he'd seen along the trail, roosting in a lodgepole pine.

He unzipped the screen door and twisted his body to crawl out of the tent, like a larvae crawling from its cocoon. There was Father Tom, squatting alongside a flat, oval-shaped rock the size of a church altar, preparing the fish he'd caught—a glistening *Oncorhynchus mykiss aguabonita* (Golden Trout) with horizontal red bands along the lateral lines on each side. At first it looked to Leo, his head still cloudy from his nap, like a piece of Chinese porcelain art a foot long.

Without breaking the spell—Father Tom approached the preparing of this dinner with the devout respect of a Catholic rite—he began to gut the trout. He held the fish firmly in one hand with the bottom facing up, and then, using his Swiss Army knife, cut upwards from the anus. Keeping the cut fairly shallow, he sliced just the skin, careful not to rip the intestines. Then he cut off the fish's head. Most of the intestines came out with it.

As he removed the remaining organs in the cut area, the eviscerated fish began looking like food to Leo.

Using his finger to scrape out the bloodline running along the spine, Father Tom then rinsed the trout with water from a Nalgene bottle.

It took some time to light the tiny stove. But once he had it fired up, Father Tom placed the trout in a tin frying pan and perched it on the stove.

A tiny narrow-mouth polyethylene bottle appeared in his palm, plucked from an inner jacket pocket. He unscrewed the cap and drizzled olive oil onto the frying fish. Within seconds, the odor of fish and olive molecules ignited Leo's olfactory glands. His body felt oddly numb, and his nose became the center of his universe. He'd never smelled anything so wonderful. Perhaps the odor of pine, the glacier-purified air at 11,000 feet, the salt and pepper granite, brooding Mount Emerson—a whirligig of sensory input—contributed to his amplified sense of the world.

Father Tom flipped the tiny fish with a plastic fork and cooked it a little longer. He removed the pan from the fire and placed it between the two men on a small flat rock.

He'd still not made eye contact with Swift; he was focused on his work. Hadn't made eye contact since they'd left the trail and abandoned each other's company for their naps. He closed his eyes and opened his palms, turning them heavenward.

"Full of joy and thankfulness, we say thank you, Lord, from the bottom of our hearts. We look at the food that has been offered up from one of your beautiful lakes, we look into the faces of those that love us and whom we love." Father Tom opened his eyes. Leo looked at him intently; Tom returned the gaze with a smile.

Then they each reached for their forks and took turns stabbing at the fish, placing the tiny morsels into their mouths.

While Father Tom and Doctor Swift ate their dinner, savoring every bite, a spectacle appeared over the nearby lake. At the very moment when the sun dropped behind Mount Humphreys and a splash of Alpenglow ignited the tip of the peak fiery-orange; at the moment when Leo reached for the flask filled with fine Scotch to wash down their savory golden trout bits—the scene unfolded.

Millions of mosquitoes alighted from a clump of stunted pine, swarmed in a cloud over the lake and skimmed the surface. As they did so, trout erupted to the surface and gulped them down, their evening feast, causing the lake to bubble and sparkle like a thousand miniature exploding suns as the water caught the reddening sunlight. Leo could understand why someone, like John Muir, or perhaps even himself, would want to spend a life out there. It wasn't the isolation. It was the sense of mystery.

After much sipping of Scotch, they discussed whether transubstantiation is meaningful in a post-Enlightenment world.

"Father Tom. What do I say to someone who asks me if Catholics truly believe that wine is the blood of Christ?" asked Leo, exasperated. "They look at me as if I were a vampire, or a cannibal, or simply insane."

"Yes, I know what you mean, Leo," he replied, shaking his head. "Some people claim that the wine actually undergoes a molecular transformation after the consecration by the celebrant." He shook his head a second time, smiling. "I understand the confusion. The words of Jesus seem plain enough. 'This is my body. This is my blood.' 'Unless you eat the flesh of the son of man and drink his blood, you do not have life in you.' 'My flesh is real food, my blood is real drink.' At the same time, a literal interpretation seems repugnant to reason. I get it."

"Then what do you say?"

"You say to them, Leo, that there is more to reality than the physical. Not everything is visible. In the case of the Eucharist, there is something new there that was not before. God's presence is real even though it is spiritual and not carnal."

"Well, it seems to me," said Leo, "if he'd used a simile—my flesh is like real food—might've ended the debate. Might've prevented the Thirty Years War, the Protestant Reformation, Lord knows what else."

Then after reflection Father Tom smiled broadly, his teeth glowing Cheshire Cat-like in the moonlight. "I've been thinking."

"What's that?"

"You aren't going home, are you? After we leave here."

Leo was silent as he sipped his Scotch.

"Tell me what you're feeling, Leo."

Again, silence.

"You're welcome to stay at the rectory."

Leo shifted his haunches uncomfortably on his stone chair.

"No, it won't be a problem. If you need a new place to start over, well ..." Father Tom said this with great finality: "You can have Monsignor's room."

"Why can't I live like John Muir? In the wilderness?"

This was not an unreasonable query. Muir climbed a number of mountains, including Cathedral Peak and Mount Dana, hiked an old trail down Bloody Canyon to Mono Lake. He sometimes hiked a dozen miles a day in his beloved Sierras. Carrying few provisions, his strict Calvinist upbringing helping him to live in a constant state of austerity, Muir traversed the mountains living on berries and other edible plants. He built a cabin in Yosemite and lived there for years.

"But thank you for your offer, Father. I'm not too sure where I belong at this point. I guess you could say I'm in Purgatory."

"Leo, look. You know I'll help you. Any way I can. The Church will help you. You can stay at the rectory."

Tom's eyes met Leo's searching stare. And then Leo's face collapsed as he fought back a sob. It wasn't so much a sob as a catching of his breath.

"You're going to be okay, Leo," Father Tom said, placing his hand on his friend's shoulder. And then he leaned over and hugged his friend. Leo wasn't alone in feeling deep gratitude. Leo knew that if he spoke, he would cry, and so he did not speak. He needed Father Tom's presence, and that was all.

Later that night, tucked away in his sleeping bag, Leo closed his eyes and fell into a deep sleep, satiated by food and friendship, his belly full of trout, boiled freeze-dried noodles, and Aberfeldy 21 Scotch whiskey. In his dream—sometimes dreams were so vivid, so real, that when he awakened he would struggle to convince himself that consciousness is real life—in this dream Janice, looking like Sandro Botticelli's Venus, emerged from Desolation Lake, standing naked on an open, pink, vaginal-looking scallop shell, illuminated only by blue moonlight, and then walking on the water, Jesus-like, towards him. Her hands reached out in a gesture of longing, palms turned heavenward. But then suddenly she shrank to the size of a trout and lay sizzling in a frying pan, her scaly body floating in a thin layer of bubbling olive oil, a single eye staring hectic red at Leo, as he began to eat her.

43

Chandler and Paul left the headmaster's office. Chandler had answered as best she could the lieutenant's probing questions (since she knew nothing whatsoever about her father, the meeting was brief). She promised to keep him informed of any news pertaining to Doctor Swift's whereabouts.

The administration building, built in the seventies, perched wide and squat at the top of the hill, looked a bit like a discarded shipping box. But the rest of the campus was designed (so states the school's website) to convey "a sense of the magical, a peaceful oasis from the harsh realities of the outside world," making the admin building something of an anachronism: old-school boxy and entirely functional doesn't seem to jive with magical. The lunch table and foliage green umbrella–dotted courtyard below, where the students and faculty gathered for lunch—even though it was July, summer school and sports activities attracted students from as far west as Oak Park and as far east as Azusa; as far north as Santa Clarita and as far south as Manhattan Beach—was bucolic. Basically, the place resembled a small liberal arts college or a country club rather than a typical public high school campus.

They stopped at the top of the twin flights of steps leading down to the courtyard—the main congregating point, the pulsating heart of the campus. The two cement stairways run in opposite directions to each other, spiraling downward like the twin strands of DNA.

"Can we stay a few minutes?" asked Chandler. Paul wrapped an arm across her shoulders.

"Sure. Whatever you want."

"The way I see it, my father has worked here all these years."

"Right. I get it."

"It's like I feel his spirit here, or something like that. Is that weird?"

"It's a spiritual thing—his presence."

As they descended the steep steps—Chandler taking one strand of the stairway while Paul took the other—they kept their eyes on each other. If they weren't in close physical proximity, they had to be visually linked—it was a "spiritual thing." Paul smiled and waved, and Chandler waved back.

They both arrived at the bottom of the steps at the same moment. Paul's arm immediately returned to her shoulders, and he gave her a hug.

"Did you notice? Most of the students prefer to take *your* stairway," he said, watching kids pass by her on the way up.

"Yeah," she replied. "Both ways are the same distance, I think. But they use the left side."

"A case of herd mentality?" he wandered, shaking his head.

As they slowly navigated their way through the maze of tables and the grazing herd, Chandler thought to herself, *He's real. My father ate lunch here. This was his world.*

She and Paul were acutely aware that they stood out: they were unfamiliar faces, strangers—outsiders. Students seemingly gave them little notice, but Chandler sensed that she and Paul were being scrutinized covertly. To the student body, they were outsiders, visitors to their isolated "peaceful oasis," non-club members and therefore objects of curiosity.

A tall, thin man, with a thick mop of reddish hair and equally crimson goatee—perhaps Irish?—in his late fifties, wearing a priest's white collar and thick-lensed glasses, which gave him a James Joycean myopic look, approached them with a jaunting gate. He smiled broadly and extended his hand to Chandler and said:

"Hi, there. I'm Father Ralph."

He shook Chandler's then Paul's hands while they could only stare perplexed at the gregarious man, who seemed immensely, even cartoonish-ly, delighted to speak with them. As an ambassador representing the school, it is his job to make visitors feel welcomed.

"I'm sorry. You're Chandler, and you're Paul, do I have it right?"

"I don't think I know you," said Chandler cautiously.

The students chattered within their small cliques at the nearby tables, and a line began to form at the entrance to the cafeteria. Fourth period, a common "free" or what they call an "X-period," had just begun.

"I just came from the headmaster's office. Came in right after you left," he said cheerfully. "He tells me everything, you know." Chandler shot a glimpse at Paul, who frowned. "Please. Can I get you some lunch?"

"Thank you, Father. But no. We just thought we'd look around, then go," said Chandler, although she failed to mask her curiosity entirely.

"Oh! Okay. No problem! I just thought you'd like to know."

She waited. "Know what?"

"I know your dad," he said proudly.

"What?" asked Chandler, looking confused. Her throat constricted. *Surreal* was her first thought. Then: *My father was dead to me. He didn't exist. He was, then never was. And now I walk where he walked, and talk to a man who had spoken to my father. No, he's real. My father was and is real.*

"You're a friend of his?" she asked, wiping quickly at her eyes.

"Well, yes, a friend, although your dad isn't easy to get to know. The students love him, mind you!" He scanned the courtyard, and he waved to a student in the distance. "I'm the chaplain here, you see. We're an Episcopal school, did you know that? Technically speaking, anyway. At least we were in the early days. Before World War II. Lofton's really a secular school, hardly anybody goes to chapel anymore, and pretty much half the students are Jewish, but they keep me on mostly for tradition's sake. And for the spiritual needs of *some* of the children and faculty." He turned and looked up the hill behind him. "You see the chapel?—Saint Wilfred's? Been there since 1928, at the very top, behind the admin building." And then he added: "Sadly, a bit deserted these days."

Chandler looked at him quizzically, glancing at his collar. "You're not an English teacher, how—"

"How do I know your dad?" He smiled, relishing this moment to share all that he knew. "We have a little service, really sweet, every Tuesday at 7 a.m., up there at Saint Wilfred's—a very old tradition. Readings from the gospels, Eucharist, prayer. At seven-thirty, before first-period class. You dad sometimes joined us in the chapel. Not every week, but from time to time. There are about six of us faithful." He smiled proudly. "Six out of a faculty of over forty. I'll take that!"

"I don't know anything about my father," said Chandler.

"Look," said Father Ralph, suddenly quite serious, leaning closer into Chandler conspiratorially. She remembers now that she could smell his minty breath. "I think I know where you can find your dad," he said in a low voice.

Chandler blinked, waiting without breathing, brushing her hair back with the fingers of her left hand while gripping Paul's with her right.

"Don't worry. I haven't said a thing to the boss, or to anybody," he said, clicking his tongue. "I wouldn't betray your dad. Are you kidding? He's a *good* man. And he was my friend."

"I don't know if he was a good man. I don't know anything about him. My mother acted like he was a monster," she said, then shook her head. "It doesn't matter." She brightened. "It makes me happy to hear what you said."

"I'm telling the *truth!*" he insisted. "He was a good man, Chandler, and so God help me."

Chandler took a deep breath and let it out slowly. "I have to say, Father, I don't know if I really want to talk to him now that I'm here. I don't know what I'd say. Honestly, I might yell at him," she said evenly. "I don't know this man."

"I understand. *Completely*. You can see him when you're ready. Or not at all!"

But then, as Chandler turned her gaze to the students at a nearby table who were huddled together watching a video on an iPhone, their heads pressed together as they squinted in the sunlight, Father Ralph looked all around to see if they were in earshot of anyone, and feeling safe enough he said:

"I spotted your dad at a funeral Mass for Monsignor McGillis, a friend of mine for many years. I've known him, I think maybe thirty years. A little Catholic church down by the beach. Great parish, mind you! Your dad was there. I'm telling you! I saw him. Right there, in the flesh, across the parking lot. I don't think he saw me. Wonderful homily, it was. Father Tom is one of the best speakers in the archdiocese. I didn't get a chance to track your dad down after the proceedings. So many people! But it was him. I'm sure of it. It was him, all right."

He extended his hand to Chandler, who hesitated, then took it. The father's warm, bony hand enveloped hers, and gripped it reassuringly.

"I think there's a chance—albeit a small one, but I have a feeling, and I'm quite intuitive about these things. If you go to the parish office, ask around, they might be able to help you." Then he added for emphasis: "You can finally meet your dad."

"You think they'll talk to me?" asked Chandler, incredulous. "He's *hiding*, right? The police are looking for him. We read about it online."

"*Think?*" he asked looking keenly at her.

She met his gaze.

"They'll talk to you because you are Leo Swift's daughter. I am certain of that."

It struck her at that moment that she was experiencing an unfamiliar feeling. Whatever it was, it warmed her.

44

Once Swift entered the wilderness all sense of time was determined by the sun's position in the sky. He did not own a smartphone and in any case, there were no cellphone towers in the Sierras. Moreover, he did not own a watch. He liked it that way. He could lose himself more easily in the wilderness. Or, rather, find himself. He recalled what Thoreau had instructed: "You must live in the present, launch yourself on every wave, find your eternity in each moment." Now that Lofton Academy had cut him free and he was settled in Humphreys Basin, he was living by Thoreau's philosophy—living in the moment.

By the time the sun crested the nearest peak on the third morning of their adventure, Leo cared about nothing except the beauty of the placid, Edenic surroundings and his friendship with Father Tom, who was off somewhere by himself taking photos of wildflowers with his beloved Olympus TG-3. Leo would never return to L.A. If he did, he'd be arrested and all his retirement money would be gobbled up by a lawyer. But assuming he were exonerated of the school's claims, what school would hire old Leo Swift? What school would risk its reputation, even if the lawyer succeeded in clearing him of any charges? The stigma would remain, indelible as his Sharpie marker's annotations on a student paper: the stigma of having been arrested for a crime so ignominious in the eyes of society that he would forever be branded a leper.

No. He'd lost his job at Lofton. His beloved students—gone. Frannie, Zack Henninger, all seventy of his students—gone.

Earlier, over freeze-dried morning coffee and gummy instant oatmeal, he'd talked to Father Tom about it—basic, existential questions. Why leave the rest of the world behind? What did the hermetic life offer him? Stereotypes and assumptions? Spiritual awakening? A feeling of safety? Loneliness?

Out here, in the woods, he would never feel alone. He was in the presence of God, he sincerely believed. He would step into the trees and walk away from everyone. He would sacrifice everything "of the world" for complete autonomy and freedom in the woods.

To the rest of the world he would cease to exist.

Leo's musings were hardly unique. Famous nature-lovers and recluses abound in history. John Muir returned to his beloved Sierras again and again to "feed on God's inexhaustible spiritual beauty," as he put it, writing in his journal. Thoreau famously spent two years, two months, and two days at Walden, living in his tiny cabin that he built himself. "I went to the woods because I wished live deliberately, to front only the essential facts of life, and see if I could not learn what it had to teach, and not, when I came to die, discover that I had not lived," he explains in his book, a reflection on simple living.

Then there's the more recent case of Christopher Knight, the "North Pond hermit," who survived 27 years alone in the Maine woods until the police arrested him for stealing supplies from cabins in the area. He loved the trees that kept him hidden and spoke of a nature goddess. After his arrest, he claimed that there was only one instance during all his years of solitude that he spoke with another human being: he'd said "Hi" to a hiker he'd encountered on a path near his hidden campsite.

At the age of 21, Tenzin Palmo swapped her job as a London librarian for a life as a nun in a monastery in India. Still feeling unfulfilled, surrounded by men who made her feel excluded, she moved to a cave, and spent twelve years there. "I moved into the cave when I was thirty-three and was very happy," she wrote. "In most places in the world it would be impossible to feel so safe and confident in isolation."

There are numerous such Christian hermits in history, beginning with Anthony the Great who, around 270 AD, heard a Sunday sermon arguing that perfection could only be achieved by selling one's possessions, giving the proceeds to the poor, and escaping deep into the desert to seek complete solitude.

And, of course, Christ himself went into the wilderness for forty days to seek understanding and meaning.

But these men and women were not outlaws, like Leo, who sought both spiritual fulfillment but also asylum from the law. Perhaps more romantic are the cowboy outlaws who evaded the law by fleeing into the hills. Robert Leroy Parker, better known as Butch Cassidy, had a history of vanishing into the wilderness with his loot from train robberies and bank heists. He fled to Robber's Roost, for example, near Capital Reef National Park, and Hole in the Wall in Wyoming for years before he finally went to Patagonia with his friend, the Sundance Kid, in 1901.

For Leo, the alternative path, rather than escaping into the Eastern Sierras, where chances of long-term survival are slim, would be to return to Los Angeles. If Leo were to revisit civilization, he would have to reinvent himself. No longer "Professor Swift," he would be branded—what, exactly? "Killer" of that Lofton girl? Simply "Criminal"? "Sexual predator"? How exactly would society react if he were to be found guilty?

Jail would not do.

"God sometimes calls some men to dedicate their

lives to serving the Church," suggested Father Tom as he sipped his tepid coffee. Leo's face was taut with brooding. "Like me, some men are configured to this calling through the sacrament of Holy Orders," he said. "It's a thought, anyway," he added almost whimsically, tilting his head to the side as he watched a foraging ant crawl up the side of his plastic cup.

Leo's initial response was surprise. "What exactly are you saying, Father?"

"I get the feeling that you're not looking to go back into teaching. Which is a shame. I know that's how you define yourself. As Leo Swift: *Teacher.*"

Leo pursed his lips tightly for a moment. "I'm done with teaching. I'm never going back."

Father Tom gave a small sigh. "I'm reminded of a passage in the Scriptures: There was a man named Nicodemus who said to Jesus, 'Rabbi, we know that you have come from God as a teacher; for no one can do these signs that you do unless God is with him'. And Jesus answered him: 'Truly, truly, I say to you, unless one is born again he cannot see the kingdom of God.'"

Leo Swift looked off, as if measuring the distance from where they sat to the peak of Mount Humphreys.

Father Tom ventured: "Can I be completely candid with you, Leo?"

Blinking, as if returning from a trance: "Yes, of course, Father."

"It's not easy for me to say this." Father Tom stared

into his coffee cup as if searching for the right words. "But, maybe the time has come for you to serve others in a new way—"

"I can't go back. Simple as that," said Leo definitively.

"Please hear me out. You can't spend the rest of your life hiding out here in the wilderness, Leo. Doing your version of John Muir. Henry David Thoreau. An anchoritic monk. Some romantic notion you have of banishment." He eyed Leo closely, although there was no sarcasm in his tone at all. He was a big, sturdy man, with eyes fixed and unyielding , but he spoke from the heart and with compassion. "No. That won't do. No running away for you, Leo. You must absolve yourself of all wrongdoing in a court of law. Simply put. And then, when it's all over and your name is cleared—which it *will* be—you take a job with the Church." He smiled, adding impishly, "I'm spelling it out for you, Leo!"

Leo was about to drink the rest of his coffee from his plastic bowl—which had just been used to cradle his oatmeal—when he noticed that the bowl was empty. He placed it down on the flat chunk of granite that served as their coffee table.

"So. What about the diaconate?" asked Father Tom simply.

"A deacon."

"I'm sure of it!" Father Tom then launched into an

explanation of the intricate details of the process to a bewildered Leo:

"Okay. There are two stages of preparation before ordination, the aspirant path and the candidate path."

"I don't —"

"Once accepted by the bishop," continued Father Tom, undeterred, "the aspirant level of formation begins — prayer, study, spiritual direction, interviews with the formation director, and continued parish life. I've looked into this carefully. According to canon law, candidates for the permanent diaconate must be at least twenty-five years old if unmarried and, if married, at least thirty-five. Married men also need their wives' consent. An unmarried man like you, once he's ordained to the diaconate, he commits himself to a life of celibacy."

He stopped to study Leo for his reaction, which was at this point a blank.

"I think you'd make a fine deacon. Really, I do! Look, Leo. You're a teacher by nature. And you're an idealist. You give to others — it's your nature! In your case, knowledge, that's what you give. A spiritual life may be your calling. No! Think about it. If it all works out, if you are admitted to the program, and *if* you complete the one-year aspirancy period, as I said, followed by a four-year candidacy period — well, all will be well."

"Five years?"

"What do you think? A possibility? Is that a maybe?"

"Wait a second. Doesn't the Church have enough problems? How could they ordain a man like me? All those scandals around priests molesting children? Me, fired for touching a student's knee?"

"Yes, Leo, the Church most certainly has had its share of controversy over the past two thousand years, and lately it's been under siege. But like a ship that's blown off course by a storm, the Church will right itself. Always does, has for two thousand years, again and again." He smiled as he waved off a mosquito, the first attacker of the day. "I'll handle the politics. The archbishop and I are friends. Trust me. He'll hear me out."

Leo Swift was silent.

Father Tom responded to Leo's muteness with a chuckle. "Nothing to worry about, Leo. No need to say anything," he said, patting his friend's knee. "No pressure at all. It's just a thought. Something to think about. To pray over."

Leo felt deeply moved by his friend's offer, and he knew right then that he loved this man.

For the moment, anyway, he felt something resembling happiness.

45

Paul guided his Suzuki to a stop in the church parking lot, revving the engine one last time, as if clearing the bike's throat of exhaust, and shut it off. The contrast between the snarl of the bike's engine and the hush of the deserted parking lot once Paul cut off the engine was acute.

Chandler, straddling the seat as she hugged his leather-jacketed back, wearing another leather jacket he'd lent her, unfastened her helmet strap. They dismounted like urban cowboys, removed their helmets and tucking them under their arms. They looked up at the large white cross on the hill behind the church that marked the location like an arrow on a Google map.

Chandler unzipped her jacket and followed Paul to the rectory.

The parish manager, Harriet, looked to be a woman in her seventies. She was short and pudgy, resembling the outer shell of a Russian doll, and had short-cropped grey hair and a rosy face that beamed brightly when Paul and Chandler entered the office.

"Hello!" she said, retrieving a page from the copier. "May I help you?"

"I hope so," said Paul.

The woman, still clutching the sheet of paper, quickly scanned him from head to toe—his Ray-Bans perched on top of his head, the twin curves of the lenses protruding like Devil's horns, his charismatic smile, the leather motorcycle jacket, his lanky, tall frame, the cowboy boots.

"I'm Paul. This is Chandler."

The woman placed the copied letter on her desk and took his extended hand, still smiling.

"I'm Harriet."

The friendly woman gave them her full attention, friendly in a way that made Chandler feel as if she were a visiting dignitary from a remote land.

"My father is Leo Swift," said Chandler perhaps too quickly. "Dr. Leopold Swift. He's my biological father," she added with just a smidgeon of pride. "I'd like to talk to him." Her face looked flushed and there was a roaring in her ears.

The woman brightened. "Oh, yes. I know Leo. Leo's a parishioner."

Chandler stiffened, pressing closer to Paul.

"He attended the R.C.I.A. meetings here in the rectory meeting room. The Rite of Christian Initiation for

Adults? He was welcomed into the church not long ago."

Paul squeezed Chandler's hand and said, "We were hoping we could find him here, or you might at least know where he's staying."

"Oh, I see. It won't be easy," the woman said, suddenly downcast. "I'm sorry. He and Father Tom went backpacking together. Father is on vacation," she added, brightening again. "Is there anything *I* can help you with?"

Her heart racing, her face strained, her lips quivering—Chandler spoke to the woman in an earnest tone. She was resolute. "It's important that I talk to my dad. *Really* important. Do you have any idea how I can find him?"

Harriet searched Chandler's eyes for a moment, eyes that were glistening and wide, and she said at last, "All I can say is, there's no way even I can reach him. Even in an emergency. They're hiking in the mountains where there's no cellphone access. All I know is he's somewhere in the Sierras and that he'll call me on Saturday, when they climb out."

"It's Wednesday," said Paul wistfully, his eyes meeting Chandler's.

The woman continued, suddenly alert: "Is there anything wrong? Is this an emergency?" Her smile transformed into a look of concern. "Father did tell me that in an emergency, I could contact the park ranger's office in Bishop. They'd have information on which campsite they're at, when they're coming out. Or you can check in with them yourselves."

Paul's eyebrows raised. He looked at Chandler, who met his gaze. "Thank you," he said. "That helps."

"I hope everything is all right."

"We'll be fine," Paul said as he reached for the door. And then, as an afterthought: "Do you happen to know what car Father Tom drives?"

"Hmmm," she said, tapping her left temple with two fingers. Then, livening: "Well, I'm pretty sure it's a Nissan. I pay the bills on it, so I should know. Oh, gosh. The memory's not as it was." Then she brightened. "I know! An Xterra. A red one."

"Could we leave a little message for Mr. Swift?" asked Chandler.

"Yes, of course." The woman handed Chandler a small notepad from her desk and snatched a pen from a coffee cup sprouting a bouquet of pens and pencils.

"Thank you," said Chandler as she took the pen and began to write. She chose her words carefully as she jotted a note, and then handed it to the woman.

She thanked the woman and Paul opened the door for Chandler.

Outside in the parking lot, as they fitted their helmets over their heads, Paul turned to Chandler:

"What did you say in your note?"

"Just 'Hope to talk with you' and I signed it 'Your daughter Chandler.' I gave him your cell number."

"He won't know who Chandler is."

"True. But *daughter* should get his attention, don't you think?"

She fastened the helmet and waited for him to mount the motorcycle. Once he'd settled into the seat, she climbed on behind him and scissored his hips with her thighs, bracing herself as he revved up the engine, a roaring sound that never ceased to startle her with its power as it violated the serene silence of the church grounds.

She then said, decisively: "Bishop."

"What?" he shouted over the thunder of the engine, twisting his body and turning his head to look at her. "When? You mean right *now?*"

"Sure. Why not?" She raised her eyebrow.

He nodded, revving the engine and releasing the brake.

She would say nothing more until they parked the motorcycle at the White Mountain Ranger Station in Bishop.

46

They headed north on a day hike and would be back by lunch. Father Tom was carrying a simple, inexpensive JanSport daypack that reminded Swift of his students' ubiquitous (and much more expensive) backpacks, stuffed with laptop, text books, phones, and God only knows what that they toted around campus. Burdened with these distended bags, the students always reminded Leo of foraging ants carrying food many times their own weight back to their nests. In Father Tom's case, his pack held two Nalgene water bottles and two bags of Trader Joe's trail mix.

They headed in the general direction of Packsaddle, but their wanderings were mostly aimless—guided only by the Holy Spirit, if you will. Father Tom stopped periodically to examine the rocks. Granite, diorite and monzonite, formed when molten rock cooled far beneath the surface of the earth. He explained to Leo, "Granitic rocks have speckled salt and pepper appearance because they contain various minerals including quartz, feldspars and micas," as Leo listened attentively and occasionally nodded.

At one point they found themselves lost in a waist-high thicket of shooting star wildflowers that engulfed them in a wonderful cloud of violet.

As the morning progressed, Father Tom grew slightly concerned as the clouds in the sky thickened. Thunderstorms can hit with terrifying suddenness and then clear up just as quickly, and the shooting-stars flowers, tall and nimble, were swaying like nervous first-graders waiting for a school bus on the first day of school. There were a few light sprinkles. An ominous sign.

They hiked for two hours, stopping occasionally to examine rocks and to photograph flowers. For Father Tom, everything had a presence and a sign. God in each rock and tree. But as the sky thickened overhead, the clouds rapidly growing denser by the moment, he stopped to read the cloud patterns, as if they were a source of divination—like tea leaves, coffee grounds, or wine sediments. The clouds grouped, pulled apart, then regrouped, shapeshifting like mythological creatures.

To an experienced hiker in the Sierras, they were sacred talismans to be heeded.

47

Rain battered them as they raced up 395, thighs clasping the motorcycle seat like nutcrackers. Fortunately, Paul had an extra pair of goggles for Chandler, but at this speed the raindrops stung their exposed faces.

They decided not to stop for any reason—they were on a mission—except to refuel and use the gas station restrooms. Soaked, tired, cold, they sped on, the Suzuki's engine shrieking, the Owens Valley lake now dry from the state's persistent draught, the rain and wind a roar. They passed endless volcanic rock and drove through the towns of Cartago and Olancha. Mount Whitney and the mountains surrounding Death Valley are visible from 395, but Paul and Chandler failed to take notice. They passed slowly through Lone Pine with its tightly enforced speed limit of 35 miles an hour, but shot by the Manzanar National Historic Site, the concentration camp where Japanese Americans were imprisoned during World War II. None of this registered with them. They raced by the small Fort Independence Indian reservation and the Tinemaha Reservoir, then slowed down to pass through Big Pine, where due north from Westgaard Pass lies the Ancient Bristlecone Pine Forest, home to trees as old as the Great Pyramids.

They rode in a trance, pummeled by the elements, travelers on an asphalt River Lethe, no longer concerned with the past but only with their destination. The rain came down large and persistent.

Once they pulled into the White Mountain Ranger Station and Visitor Center parking lot, they lost no time parking the bike and dismounting, their bodies stiff and drenched after the three-hour ride. Chandler, shivering, hunched under the rainfall, her hair matted and drips falling from her nose, followed Paul, who was also hunched forward, into the building.

They approached the ranger on duty, a young, sturdy woman wearing her green ranger's pants and grey shirt uniform, her hair tied back in a pragmatic bun, and they told her their story. Her father was camping in the wilderness somewhere. She had to find him—it was an emergency.

"Of course, finding your dad will be worse than finding a needle in a haystack," the ranger said gravely. "Forget that cliché. More like finding a pine needle in the Sierras." The woman immediately realized, after seeing the severity of Chandler's expression, that this wasn't the time for light-hearted wit.

She brought out her reservation binder and opened it. "What'd you say your dad's name was?"

Swift's name wasn't listed as the "group leader," but Father Tom's was—Gerbajs—as he had purchased the permit. The ranger showed Chandler the listing, which included Father Tom's name, the church's address, and the parish phone number; the name of the trail, along with entry and exit dates; and the description of the car at the trailhead—a Nissan Xterra.

She also gave Paul detailed directions. "From Bishop, you take Highway 168 east. You head toward North Lake at the junction with North Lake Road. There's a parking area there, just before the North Lake campground. You can camp there for the night and head out in the morning. The trail follows the north fork of Bishop Creek. Piute Pass is about five miles from the trailhead. Would you like to purchase a day pass?"

Paul said he would, and she asked them to return in the morning. It would be too dangerous to hike after dark, after all. Paul promised her they'd return in the morning, at 8:00 when the office opened.

But Chandler had no intention of waiting until tomorrow to join her father.

Whoever he is.

48

Leo was worried. Father Tom had lost the trail leading back to camp.

It wasn't a man-made trail to begin with. Not even close. During the Great Depression, the Civilian Conservation Corps worked in the parks to build and improve campgrounds, trails, buildings, and other facilities. The trails they made were wide, level, and well maintained. But the trail Father Tom and Leo were following that day was merely a thin ribbon of dirt, no more than two or three feet wide, plowed and worn down by a variety of critters: golden-mantled ground squirrel, mule deer, black bear, mountain lion, marmot, pika, white-tailed jack rabbit.

As sheets of rain blanketed the meadow, Father Tom searched the area for the elusive trail, his hand forming a gable over his eyes to shield the rain. His floppy hat had blown to the ground and he hoped to spot it. He appeared uncharacteristically worried.

"Wait here," he instructed as he stooped to retrieve his hat.

Leo scanned the bleak landscape worriedly. "Wait! We have a compass, right? Why don't we just head in a straight line due south back to camp? Do we need to follow the trail? The terrain seems tenable enough."

"No. We *need* the trail," Father Tom replied severely.

Leo nodded. He was worred: his friend was a wise man, a father figure, a protector, and Leo had never seen Father Tom looking so concerned.

Leo spotted a heap of granite boulders forming a slight canopy and took refuge, squatting under the stony outcrop. He watched his friend become engulfed by the wet grey, scouring the area as if he'd lost a priceless gem in the dirt, his face and eyes protected precariously by his wide-brimmed hiking hat. Feeling helpless, Leo waited, shivering as he batted away rain droplets. He scanned the sky for an encouraging sign, but everything was hoary grey.

When he turned around to look for Tom, his friend had vanished.

Between the assailing rain and the dimming light, Leo's vision had diminished dramatically. He could see no more than a few yards. The bleakness of the terrain, a feeling of abandonment, the utter isolation. A horrible creeping loneliness set in.

All his thoughts were obliterated except one: What would he do if Father Tom failed to return?

The idea that Father Tom might not come back struck Leo hard. There were many cracks and booms of lightning zigzagging and forming silvery cracks in the sky like broken glass. From somewhere deep within his unconscious self, Dante's words percolated up to his lips. He hadn't read *The Inferno* in years. He was surprised by the power of his own memory, now kindled by the fiery elements:

> *New torments I behold, and new tormented*
> *Around me, whichsoever way I move,*
> *And whichsoever way I turn, and gaze.*
> *In the third circle am I of the rain*
> *Eternal, maledict, and cold, and heavy;*
> *Its law and quality are never new.*

Maledict. This was the moment of Leo's epiphany. How could he ever have imagined a life of wandering, a self-proclaimed exile, like Cain with his mark, forever נע ודנ — fugitive — without a home, the Sierras' pines forming his only roof? Romantic, certainly. Live like the marmots. For them it is heaven. But even *they* have families. Life out here would be fitting for a man who had spent a good portion of his adult years severing human ties, living on a whim like Thoreau, without family, as solipsistic as an ectothermic, amniote vertebrate — serpent.

He began to cry. It surprised him. He hadn't cried

in years. Even when he learned of Frannie's suicide. He could no longer envision a life alone, without his closest friend, a man for whom he felt something profound—is there a word for this feeling? Friendship? No, something deeper, wider. Holier.

Brotherhood.

He resolved then that he would return to Los Angeles, go to the police, disentangle the misconstructions regarding Frannie and Lofton. Then he would take the vows of the diaconate—five years and all—serve Father Tom, the parish, the poor, the "nobodies." He would move into the rectory—Monsignor's old room would do nicely—and live near the man who must be—for lack of a better term, since there really was no language for how he felt—a brother.

To commemorate the moment, Leo, with tears streaming, scouted the immediate area for flat rocks. He found three roughly the same size and shape, pieces of granite, flat like kitchen plates, and stacked them neatly in the clearing.

This shall be the gate of heaven, he thought, inwardly reciting the verse from Genesis in which Jacob builds a shrine and calls it "Bethel."

After forty minutes that seemed like hours, Father Tom finally emerged from the mist like a phantom, first small as a finger, a grey blur in the distance, then solid, corporeal, larger than life, smiling.

"Found it!" he said triumphantly.

They took to the trail with Father Tom leading the way. Keeping his friend's broad and sturdy back in his steady gaze, Leo trekked along the narrow path.

Two hours later, they arrived at their Desolation Lake campsite and shed their rain-soaked jackets and muddy hiking boots, each climbing into his cocoon tent to escape from the relentless rain.

They felt safe. Stable. Lucky.

But safety, stability, and luck are fleeting mental constructs in the wilderness. Ideas as fluid as a stream.

Nothing, in the end, but ebb and flow.

49

By the time Chandler and Paul arrived at the trailhead's campground, the rain had stopped, and the sun had dropped behind the mountain. The first thing they did was survey the parking lot. A dozen cars—mostly SUVs, minivans, and pickups. There were a few tidy tents already pitched in the tiny, rectangular, designated camping spaces. A few as-yet unsoiled families ate their dinners while seated at picnic tables. Bearproof trash barrels were spaced at the corners. The grounds were clean, well-maintained by the park service and conscientious visitors to God's country.

The red Xterra was off in a corner of the lot, couched between a Ford minivan and a Toyota pickup truck. They walked over to Father Tom's car and circled it as if it were a curious, avant-garde museum piece—mixed wonder and confusion. They looked inside through the driver's side window, as if hoping for a sign or proof, an unreasonable but involuntary expectation. Just for the hell of it, Paul tried the driver's side door handle.

It was unlocked.

"Well, look at that," he said, taken aback.

"Maybe they figured there was nothing for anyone to take. They took everything with them," said Chandler. "Destiny, you think?"

"I imagine many campers leave their cars unlocked so people won't break in. Saves having to replace a window." He opened the door and sat in the driver's seat. "This is a blessing, Chan. It's too dark to hike up the trail and I didn't bring a tent," said Paul. "I don't feel comfortable taking it on at night, and I don't feel like hunting down a motel in Bishop. We'll stay here. I bet your dad would be glad if he knew."

"I know something about sleeping in cars." Chandler gazed at a camper's tent nearby, neatly assembled in its ten-by-twenty-foot space.

"We'll wait for the sun to come up," said Paul. "We'll figure it out."

She pulled her leather jacket tighter around herself, zipping it up to her neck, circled the car, and opened the door. She climbed in next to Paul.

She didn't want to think about the long night ahead. Simply, she wanted to find her father, who remained, even though he was close by now, a shadow in the woods.

50

Leo and Tom crawled out of their tents after being imprisoned by the rainstorm. Its intensity was a shock to Leo, but Father Tom knew that Sierra thunderstorms are fickle things. Once gathered densely and darkly overhead, they can strike with the suddenness and savagery of a cornered rattlesnake. In the summer they often bring intense rain, hail, and lightning, particularly around one o'clock in the afternoon. Sudden changes in the weather catch many hikers by surprise, but the clouds can disperse just as quickly as they arrive, leaving the expanse scrubbed clean, benign, peaceful.

They enjoyed breathing in the pristine, rain-washed air as they made dinner, discussing over their simmering freeze-dried beef Stroganoff meal their adventures that day, although Leo left out the part about Dante's *Inferno.* They ate heartily and swigged Scotch from Tom's flask.

They tabled further discussion of Leo's future and instead traded stories. Tom recounted a story by Andre

Dubus, one of his favorite authors, but he told it with such care to detail, with such eloquent phrasing, and with such emotional might that Leo suspected his friend had a photographic memory, or something close to it. It was called "A Father's Story," and it was about a father's limitless love for his daughter. In a nutshell, the main character talks to God, and God says something back.

Leo loved James Joyce's *Dubliners* stories, so he told Tom the one he'd taught a few years ago in his junior English class: "Araby," about an unnamed young Irish boy who falls in love with his friend's sister and goes on a journey—to an exotic bazaar in Dublin—to buy a gift for the object of his desire. But she's not in love with him; in fact, she barely knows anything about him. He realizes that his pursuit of the nameless girl is a mistake, the result of his own blinding vanity. The story ends with the character returning home empty handed and ashamed. As Leo shared this tale, however, he could not quite express Joyce's exquisite control of language, and he felt as though he'd betrayed the writer in this shaky telling.

51

Paul and Chandler told stories too. In the cramped front seats of Father Tom's car, Chandler wrapped her arms around Paul, partly for warmth, entirely for love. She told him about her growing up with a bitter mother, and her mom's grief at her lover's departure—in a smothering, permanent state of mourning.

"Her being abandoned took over her life," she told Paul. "It became her identity. And then it became mine." Chandler closed her eyes, held her breath, then tried to breathe out her pain.

She knew that she had to obey her mother's command to never speak of her father under penalty of exile. In the end, she left home anyway. She exiled herself.

At the trailhead's nine-thousand-foot altitude it can get chilly at night—below freezing, even in summer—and it was uncomfortable inside the car, even though they'd moved to the backseat. Neither of them complained.

He pulled her close for a kiss.

They both were fully aware: theirs was an accidental relationship. Or perhaps it was fortuitous that they found themselves in her father's friend's car. Everything about their getting together seemed random yet functioning, like the invisible machinery of the universe. Romantics, they believed there had to be a divine intellect behind their meeting.

"When are you going to marry me, Chandler?" he asked unexpectedly. There was a long pause. A quickening of her heart beat. She couldn't believe he just said that. *Not only has he not rejected me, he actually wants to hold on to me for life.* "I love you," he added, just to cement the question. "I think it makes sense."

When she finally spoke, it wasn't what he wanted to hear: "I have to tell you something." He'd wanted an unequivocal Yes!

She didn't know if they'd recover, but she spoke brazenly: "I'm pregnant."

"I don't understand. Chandler. How can that be?"

Now it was an ugly pause.

"It happened from before I met you."

But instead of erupting in indignation, he simply looked befuddled—he had the look of someone who'd forgotten a friend's name he'd known for years. And when he regained his focus, as he looked her closely in her eyes—their faces inches apart, their bodies clutching in the backseat of a stranger's car—he said the only words that made sense: "All the more reason to get married. This child should have a mother *and* a father."

At that very moment Chandler's world was entirely remade.

52

Weary, cold, and mildly intoxicated, Father Tom and Leo returned to their tents. They were careful to remove all food from backpacks and Father Tom's daypack—trail mix, hard candy, dried fruit—and place all of it in the indestructible, bulletproof bear barrel. Using the screwdriver tool of his Swiss pocket knife, the priest tightened down the fasteners that secured the lid, and Leo volunteered to place the container a hundred yards from the camp. After making his way through an obstacle course comprised of small boulders and low shrubbery to a spot outside of camp, Leo wedged the container into a crevice in the ground and set a pile of stones atop it, forming a small pyramid of granite. But Father Tom warned him: if a bear was of a mind to get inside that barrel, he would bat the rocks away like annoying gnats.

"Well, if he's going to attack the thing," said Leo,

chuckling, "we should at least make it hard for him, right?"

"I don't know. A frustrated bear might be more of a problem than a happy one."

"In that case, maybe we should just lay the food out for him. Make it a buffet."

"Ha! Well, it might just whet his appetite."

After dutifully burying the bear barrel, Leo returned to his tent and stopped outside before entering. He took in the sky. A full moon high above, like a watchful eye in the sky. Patches of snow on the higher ridges, glowing in the moonlight. The day's rain had cleansed every inch of Creation—it was breathtaking the way it had transformed everything, thought Leo, even the air he breathed. He could imagine how someone could spend his life out there: not so much in order to escape civilization's harrowing challenges; rather, the wilderness held a mystery that encouraged inquiry.

Climbing into his tent, which he'd purposely assembled close to a house-sized boulder that acted as a windbreaker, Leo scanned the interior for food—bear bate. It was part of his nightly ritual. Then he inspected his jeans pockets for candy—there wasn't any. He slid them off his legs and rolled them up for a pillow, placing the bundle at the head of his sleeping bag. He searched the tent's interior, scouting for other food, placed a water bottle by the door, made sure the flashlight by his head was working in case he needed to leave the tent in the middle of the night to urinate. Finally, to complete the process, he laid out tomorrow's clean underwear, t-shirt, and socks at the foot of the tent, just below his sleeping bag.

After crawling into his bag, he called to Father Tom, who was twenty yards away in his own tent, which had been carefully assembled on a level strip of earth—he hated to sleep at a slant. Then, Leo looked through the window in the ceiling of the tent, a three-foot-square portal looking out on the stars that shone brightly, pinpoint sharp against the infinite black chalkboard of the night sky.

Lying in their sleeping bags, both men were aware that they needed to feel rested, to feel prepared for tomorrow's hiking.

They were exhausted. It didn't take long to doze off. They each went to sleep feeling that the day had been a victory of sorts—they'd made it back to the campsite safely, and that accomplishment was never to be taken for granted.

In a world teeming with defiant spirits, it was a victory that could never be taken away.

53

At first it sounded like a grunting pig. At least that's what Leo thought, still half-asleep. A sound of snorting and sniffing. Was it some kind of industrial-strength vacuum cleaner that was broken and faltering? Out *here*? Who would be doing housework in the mountains? Leo was somehow aware that he was dreaming—he had to be asleep.

But was he dreaming that he was dreaming?

He woke in darkness. But then he was sharply awake and propping himself up on his elbows. He'd heard something. An animal. He looked out the tiny window. The moon had moved in the sky and settled above Mt. Emerson since he'd gone to bed. There were more stars now. He could see the clearing in their campsite clearly through the mesh window.

The brightness of the moon cast the bear's shadow on the left side of Leo's tent—the side with the zipped door, which was covered by a strip of canvas to block out the wind—a shape that was sharply outlined against the canvas. Shadowplay. There was no doubt in his mind that it was a bear. The long snout. The ears. The mountainous shape. The low grunts.

Leo watched the silhouette move slowly, he himself not moving, trying not to make any noise to attract the bear's attention, although this may not have made a difference. The bear's sniffing and snorting was persistent and loud—woofs and snorts. Father Tom had warned him about what he might hear: a woofing sound meant the bear was inhaling and exhaling a number of times in rapid succession. Black bears would make a moaning sound or a loud snort when they were frightened or angry. The animal's inquisitive snout sniffed a foot away from Leo's head, with only the thin fabric of the tent separating Leo from the intruder.

The bear's shadow remained large—*unreal, like a cartoon,* thought Leo—on the tent wall. Like a movie projection. At one point, the animal bumped the tent, sending the entire structure shuddering, and Leo feared the stakes would pull out of the sandy soil.

What's the bear sniffing? He thought. *What is it that's attracting him to my tent? There's no food here, I searched the interior—*

Leo dared not switch on the flashlight, but there was enough moonlight streaming into the tent to illuminate the interior and especially himself, and he felt conspicuous, like an actor framed by a theater klieg light.

Still, the bear's snuffling and grunting.

Is Father Tom awake? Do I call out?

Alone in his flimsy little tent, with the bear pressing his nose against the fabric of the tent wall, Leo desperately scanned the floor around his sleeping bag.

And there it was.

Next to his makeshift jeans pillow was an open packet of Advil. He'd left one pill inside. The sugary candy-coated pill—red like an M&M—was all it took. Father Tom had mentioned that bears can smell even medicine. They have the most acute noses in nature and they can smell *anything.* They can smell an animal carcass twenty miles away.

Adrenalin spurted into his veins. His own senses of hearing, sight, and smell became exponentially more acute as fear mounted. His armpits were streaming. Very slowly Leo turned over in his bag and managed to maneuver to his knees. He cupped the palms of his hands together and prayed silently.

Hail Mary, full of grace, the Lord is with Thee.

He was aware that a drop of sweat ran down the back of an ear. Were his prayers heard? Was anyone listening? At this moment, Leo felt that his faith was stronger than ever before. It had to be.

Pray for us sinners now and at the hour of our death.

The bear then shuffled, lumbering and big, away from the tent, his silhouette shrinking in size on the tent wall like the Wicked Witch. Leo turned again and peeked out of the tiny overhead window.

The bear suddenly moved back into view.

It looked to be about five hundred pounds—no average specimen, to be sure. It stood ten feet from Leo's tent, midway between his tent and Father Tom's, swaying slightly as if drunk from sniffing the mountain air. It was jet black with only a narrow streak of white fur that formed a line dividing the two sides of its massive face. The black hair was the color of darkness—of death; the white was pure as glacial snow, the color of daylight—of life. But as Leo gazed fixedly at this creature, holding his breath, still praying (the Lord's Prayer), he realized that he'd encountered something much more than an earthly bear—an animal of such sublime beauty and extraordinary strength that Leo's fear was instantly supplanted by a sense of wonder.

Here was a true miracle, he thought.

Restricted by the limited space within his tent, Leo still managed to angle himself so he could watch in awe the movements of this beautiful creature, standing on four legs in front of him, and he imagined this must have been what it felt like for Moses to take off his sandals and kneel in the dust before the burning bush.

This is sacred ground and I am in the presence of the Divine.

Rather than lumber off peacefully into the darkness of the foliage nearby, the bear changed its mind—a fickle beast? A new scent?—and turned and shuffled towards Father Tom's tent.

Father Tom would never forget and leave food in his tent, thought Leo.

Is Tom still asleep? Leo wondered. Was this possible, when such a cataclysmic, axis-tilting event was taking place outside?

Leo quickly realized that the bear was intent on exploring for food in every cranny of their campsite. He further twisted his head to continue watching the bear, who then moved out of his field of vision.

Then he could hear Father Tom shouting wildly, his voice a hoarse shriek: "Go away! Go away! Go away!"

Leo quickly unzipped the tent door, pushed the drawn door cover out of the way, and climbed out into the cold. He saw the bear batting his friend's tent gently with a swinging paw, as if testing its resistance, but then it pawed the tent so fiercely that two of the tent's metal stakes rocketed out of the ground. The tent collapsed. Leo could see the shape of his friend buried under the canvass, his arms flaying, panicked.

Without hesitation, Leo began waving his own arms, frantically trying to gain the bear's attention, and screaming, "Hey! Hey! Hey! Hey!"

The bear stopped its assault on Tom's tent and pivoted suddenly to face Leo. At that moment Leo heard something else, heard small squeaking sounds, nearby. He turned to look.

A cub.

The animal was the size of a small dog, and it sat nonchalantly on the ground two feet behind Leo, playing with a plastic cup rummaged from the makeshift kitchen area of their campsite. The cub's paws swatted the cup back and forth in the dirt as if it were a new toy just found under a decorated tree on Christmas morning.

The mother bear rose up on her hind legs, swelling to eight feet tall. She towered over Leo, who looked like an elf in comparison to the monstrously large being before him. Then she charged him. He only had time to turn partway before running.

The bear overtook him in a moment, and Leo tried to fend her off with his fists, striking wildly in sheer terror. Never in Leo's life had he been involved in a fistfight, not even as a kid. But suddenly he felt surprised at his own ferocity as he slugged blindly at his attacker.

But then the bear's right paw swiped his torso below his raised left arm. Her claws shredded to curlicue bits his grey t-shirt and carved four parallel diagonal lines across Leo's exposed flesh, snagging two ribs, which snapped like twigs, puncturing a lung.

Father Tom emerged from his crumpled tent and threw his flashlight as hard as he could at the bear, and it struck and bounced off the animal's left flank. Startled (and by the grace of God?), both the bear and its cub galloped off into the dark trees, leaving Leo standing in the clearing, blood gushing from his skinned side.

He felt no pain. Nothing at all. He stood there in shock. Not even wobbling, but stone still. He was drooling reddish saliva from the corner of his mouth.

Father Tom rushed to his friend and reached out to him, just as Leo fell forward, collapsing into his arms.

54

Was he dreaming that he was dreaming?

Semi-conscious. He was back in a dream state, hiking with his father in East Fork, in the San Gabriel Mountains. He was eight years old—old enough to go hiking, alone with his father at last, although his mother argued adamantly against it. Too dangerous. He's her only son. What's more, and this gets at the heart of the issue, hikes ferried both of them out of her realm of control, and she feared chaos and lawlessness more than anything.

Leo (not his birth name, remember—I still haven't located it in any records; what information I have was relayed to me by Janice) loved and admired his father, without ever quite respecting him. He assumed that his father had done something wrong, or at least something haunting, during the war because he never talked about it. He probably killed somebody. But that would be okay, he reasoned. German spies weren't really humans, were they? According to his mom, Dad was in the OSS, a "spy-catcher" who only shared this information when pressed. But that wasn't what Leo, as a small child, disliked about his father. Rather, it was his father's cowardly acquiescence in the face of conflict. It was his resignation when embattled—especially when his mother asked about unpaid bills and his dad's some-times missing paycheck. Dad was an insurance adjuster working for the now defunct Equity Insurance Company of Omaha, and his salary was modest. But that wasn't what inflamed her wrath. The truth, which Leo didn't learn until his father had died, was that Dad was a chronic gambler, and poker was his passion. After a game of Texas Hold 'em took its cut, paychecks could barely pay the bills.

Leo knew that his father, a fellow sinner, had to obey his mother just as he had to. If you sinned in some way, you lost your voice. Mom took control.

The occasional adventures on his father's favorite hiking trails in East Fork offered welcome respite from her tireless monitoring of all their activities.

Leo could remember little of what they said on the hike. He only remembered his father helping him cross a stream by holding his hand with what seemed like a giant's grip as they walked, precisely and cautiously, like runway models, one foot daintily placed in front of the other, along the trunk of a fallen pine tree. He remembered getting caught on a rock face later on, about thirty feet above the stream, hugging the stone with all his might, acrophobia suddenly gripping him by the throat, paralyzing him: he could not go on but Dad kept talking to him—calmly. Gently. Patiently. The words he spoke did not matter. Leo heard only his dad's tone of voice, soothing and loving, as the man reached up to his son and took him firmly in his arms—his Father, his Savior—and carried him down to the riverbank, safe and sound.

He remembered his father teaching him how to swim at the local YMCA. How he would have Leo straighten stiffly like a surfboard as he held his son on the water's surface with a hand placed under his son's stomach. He remembered being told to begin the stroke he'd been taught—arms making windmill patterns, feet fluttering—and sure enough, his body glided across the width of the pool, his dad's hand still holding him up, keeping him from sinking—a horrible death, sucking in water rather than air.

Leo and his father were desperados of a sort— "partners in crime," his dad liked to say. Once they eventually returned home, they both slinked guiltily to their rooms in hopes of avoiding Mom, who would certainly scold them. They were filthy; tree branches had scratched their faces and arms; rocks had bruised their elbows and kneecaps, leaving them looking like warriors back from battle.

Or desperados.

Of all the events that transpired during his childhood — school, friends, Christmas mornings, trips to museums and libraries — it was this one experience with his dad in the San Gabriel Mountains that he remembered right now as he slipped deeper into unconsciousness on the trail below towering Mount Humphreys.

That's when it dawned on him. He's asleep. Dreaming. He must still be in his bed, at his childhood home. Mom must be somewhere. Dad would look in on him. Was he dreaming? Or was he really there, *really* there, bleeding on the trail, dreaming that he was dreaming, dying?

He'd never seen Father Tom's face looking that way before. The man had always been a wellspring of calm, of Zen-like serenity. He was Everyone's Father, always there to come to your aid, to listen to your confession. He knew everything, feared nothing, and always believed in your goodness, no matter what your sins.

Was he dreaming that he was dreaming?

Leo lay in the dirt, curled up like a fetus. Father Tom stripped off his own t-shirt and wrapped it around Leo's mangled torso to assuage the bleeding. The blood quickly soaked through the thin cotton material. As Tom secured the t-shirt, tying the ends in a knot, he pressed too hard, and a warm spurt of blood slapped him in the face. But the t-shirt managed to more or less curtail the bleeding temporarily. It was the best he could do.

Wiping the blood from his eyes with the back of a

reddened hand, he leaned close to Leo's ear. "I'm going to get you out of here. Just hang on, Leo. You're going to be okay," he insisted. And whatever it was Father told you, you knew to be true.

Quickly Father Tom dug out his pants and jacket from the folds of his decimated tent, dressed himself in a rush, laced up his boots, and plucked a hiking pole from the base of a tree. He then jogged back to Leo, who hadn't moved and looked dead to the world.

But it was only shock. His eyes were rolling. He made a gurgling sound, choking on his own spit.

"Listen, Leo," Father Tom said hoarsely, crouching down by his friend. "I'm going to get you to a hospital. I'm going to carry you out of here. It won't be easy, but I can do it. But do your part, dammit—fight to stay alive," he commanded, summoning the greatest possible effort from his friend as well as himself.

Tom stood up, fueled by adrenalin, and pulled Leo to his feet as if he were a Raggedy Anne doll. He then managed to turn around and wrestle Leo's body over his own shoulders, like a soldier rescuing a comrade on the battlefield. Taking up his hiking pole, one hand anchoring Leo to his shoulders, Father Tom lunged out of the camp, bearing his cargo as if it were merely a bigger-than-average backpack—his usual camping gear, not 145 pounds of bleeding, nearly lifeless human being.

The technical term for this extreme strength is "hysterical strength." We've all heard stories of parents lifting vehicles to rescue their children. Biologists have attributed this phe-nomenon to increases in adrenaline in the bloodstream. I suspect, however, that the source of these superhuman powers is something beyond our understanding.

Father Tom knew a shortcut. Perhaps ten years ago, he had discovered it when another hiker mentioned a bridge crossing a particularly wide stream that blocked access to a shorter trail. A careful scrutinizing of a map indeed indicated that there was a man-made bridge to the east that traversed Malbeck stream. He figured that it would take too long to hike back to the trailhead via their previous route.

The full moon still glowed bright with promise. There were horrors enough up ahead, sure enough, but Father Tom tried to remain optimistic. He followed his own advice to novice hikers: one foot in front of the other. That's all you ever think about.

The pole saved him as he descended. Kept him from toppling forward, head over heels.

All he wanted as he trekked out of their camp—a bloodied war zone—was to forget about the heavy burden draped on his shoulders, the ruined body. Instead, he focused all his attention on the dimly lit path, which, after an appallingly long half hour of excruciatingly painful uphill struggle, gave way to a precipice. Teetering on the ridge, he could see below, not too far in the distance, the promised stream, a black squiggle snaking to the south. If he found the bridge, if he were able to cross the stream—there were so many unseen *ifs* ahead—the journey back to civilization would take about three hours, maybe more, given the extra weight. Seven miles, give or take.

The sky was bright; everything around him was grey—granite and shadow. But to the south, a tiny cluster of clouds, innocuous enough at this point, stirred like gremlins.

The slope down the hillside was composed of loose chunks of granite the size of baseballs that gave easily under the weight of the two men. Father Tom lost his footing a half dozen times, but the pole always saved him. At one point he dropped to one knee, tearing open the flesh, and he cried out in pain. Undeterred, he trudged down the embankment, slowly, cautiously—it took twenty minutes before they reached the bottom.

"You okay, Leo?" he asked, his voice a wreck.

"I'm still here," he replied, his voice barely audible, unsubstantial. He'd lost so much blood that it was a Sisyphean labor to remain conscious.

But the bridge wasn't there.

"Damn it!" Father Tom shouted as he wound and squeezed his way through the low shrubbery, spidery branches tearing at the exposed flesh of his arms, until he stood at the edge of the stream. He twisted his head around to speak to his friend. "The map says there should be a bridge here. There isn't one. The bastards *lied,*" he cried, exhausted. But then, with resolve, he told

Leo: "I am *not* going back up the mountain."

He gently lifted his friend from his shoulders and placed him on the damp grass.

"Shit!" he gasped, his face contracted in pain and regret. He looked up at the sky, then looked at the ground, shaking his head. He'd never felt so much exhaustion. He rested, breathing in and out rapidly until his heart settled.

Fortunately, the stream was only knee deep at this point, and it was only about twenty yards to the other embankment. But the force of the rushing glacial water could easily sweep Father Tom's legs out from under him and carry both men away. Father Tom would probably recover his footing and make it out. It wouldn't be so easy with Leo.

"Well, I'll be your Saint Christopher," he told Leo as he grappled with his friend's limp body and replaced him on his shoulders. He then waded out into the water. "In case you never heard of him, Mister Catholic in Training, Saint Christopher carried a child," he went on, as the shock of the cold shimmied up his spine, his own voice reassuring in the silence. "Somebody he didn't know—carried him across a river—before the child revealed himself as Christ—so ol' Christopher is the patron saint of—travelers," he concluded with as much good humor as he could muster. "See? You're in—good hands, Leo!"

The force of the rushing water took him by surprise. For a moment, his boots slipped on the flattened stones paving the stream's bed, and he wobbled and jiggled precariously like a marionette on loose strings. He braced himself against the inevitable tumble by plunging the hiking pole into the gravelly riverbed on the downstream side. Then he moved to the left, scooting along carefully, pole in, pole out, pole in, pole out, the stream slamming both men and sloshing frigid water over and around them.

Drenched, Father Tom collapsed on the far embankment and slid his friend off his aching shoulders and onto the soft vegetation. It smelled sweet and wonderful.

"You still with us?" he asked Leo, mustering an upbeat tone.

"Still here," replied Leo. His voice was husky, barely audible.

Father Tom realized how intensely thirsty he felt, and he knew Leo needed water too. He knew the water in the stream could harbor giardia, which could lay him out with a nasty illness, but that would be later, after Leo was safe and patched up. Tom cupped water from the stream in his hands and offered it to his friend. Leo sipped feebly. Tom then leaned over the gushing water and took several gulps.

The path that would lead to the trailhead stretched out before Father Tom. Sandy patches among the granite slabs that lined the stream's banks on both sides were filled with wild flowers—paintbrush, columbine, tiger lily, spiraea, penstemon. A veritable garden. There were animal tracks in the mud. Hard to tell what they belonged to—his vision was faltering. Exhaustion. Exhaustion made him susceptible to dangerous thinking: they had at least three, maybe four miles to go and he was sure he couldn't make it.

He intended to survive, though, and his one good reason to survive was his friend's life, which was dwindling quickly.

He checked the makeshift bandage holding Leo's torso together; it was blood-soaked. Maybe it'd stopped bleeding. Maybe the wound wasn't so bad.

Leo moaned. "Much farther?" he asked in a whisper. All he wanted now was to wash off the blood, to take a hot shower and climb into a bed with clean white sheets.

"It's not much of a trek from here," he said dismissively. "We're gonna make it."

Father Tom laid back on the sandy bed seeking respite. Tiredness and muscle pain caused his consciousness to collapse inward.

55

He was woken by Leo's foot. He bolted upright into a sitting position. He'd fallen asleep, for who knows how long. The light was still grey, but a darker, more menacing greyness. Leo's leg had extended involuntarily, and Father Tom immediately feared the worse.

"Leo!" he cried. He scooted over to his friend's side and leaned into his face. "Leo!"

His friend's eyes opened slowly.

"I'm so sorry, Leo. I fell asleep for a second. It's okay, though. We'll get there."

Blisters on his feet, tiredness, aching legs be damned. Father Tom got up on one knee and managed, with a great struggle, to slide his friend over his shoulders, searing with pain. He stood up, grabbed the pole for support, and marched onward.

About forty-five minutes further down the trail, the real trouble began.

The path left the stream and curved up and over

273

the Piute Pass, a herculean endeavor even for a hiker in top shape. For this exhausted priest, his burden was growing heavier by the minute. And in what seemed like the eighth level of Dante's hell, Father Tom slowly descended the far side of the mountain on a series of zigzagging switchbacks that were designed to lessen the angle of the incline but required sure footing, hiking expertise, and the conscientious use of hiking poles.

Father Tom talked to Leo incessantly, hoping to distract himself from his own horrible, despairing thoughts and keep Leo from losing consciousness.

But the time came when he asked Leo a question—he doesn't remember what the question was, as he was feeling delirious at this point—and Leo did not answer.

The rainclouds Tom had seen earlier suddenly closed in above. The rain began to fall in torrents, a surprise as Tom had stopped thinking about the clouds long ago. The trail's visibility was poor and the ground became slippery, making progress even more difficult.

Ironically, it was on this level-but-navigable ground that the tendon snapped.

Tom felt his Achilles tendon—which had held up well under extraordinary duress so far—go. He could swear he heard a popping noise, like a stepped-on twig in the forest. Or a champagne cork popping. But there was no celebrating this turn of events. With his friend still gripping his back like a baby orangutan upon its mother, he collapsed onto the ground in a heap.

The pain was paralyzing.

56

Father Tom managed to crawl under a rocky outcropping, dragging his friend with him. At first he thought he could tame the pain. Then he tried to stand up and his leg gave out from under him and the pain kicked in with excruciating intensity. He cursed his bad luck. There was no going anywhere.

The rain continued its onslaught. He lay back down and looked at Leo, whose head was resting on his right thigh as if it was as a pillow. When Tom placed his right hand on Leo's head, Leo flinched and murmured "Oh!" He sweated and his body shook. "I'm sorry, Father Tom," he said.

Then he closed his eyes.

"We're going to make it out of here, Leo. I'm going to pray for us. You keep praying too, okay, Leo?"

At that moment, as the falling rain pummeled their legs and Tom cradled his friend's head in his arms, he was about to begin when he remembered that he still had the olive oil from dinner. He burrowed into his pocket with his left hand and felt for the bottle; yes, there it was. And it still held the sacred oil he'd used for frying the trout. He squeezed the plastic top between thumb and forefinger and twisted it off.

He placed the bottle on a flat stone that he served as an altar and raised both extended hands over it in a gesture of blessing. He looked heavenward and said, "Lord God, loving Father, you bring healing to the sick through your Son Jesus Christ. Hear us as we pray to you in faith, and send the Holy Spirit upon this oil, which nature has provided to serve the needs of men."

He made the sign of the cross over the oil and continued. "May your blessing come upon all who are anointed with this oil, that they may be freed from pain and illness and made well again in body, mind, and soul. Father, may this oil be blessed for our use in the name of our Lord Jesus Christ, who lives and reigns with you forever and ever. Amen."

Father Tom then lifted up the bottle and tilted it so that a few drops of oil dribbled onto the fingers of his right hand. He made the sign of the cross on Leo's forehead, using the index and middle fingers pressed tightly together, and prayed. "Through this holy anointing may the Lord in his love and mercy help you with the grace of the Holy Spirit. May the Lord who frees you from sin save you and raise you up."

Leo suddenly opened his eyes. He smiled and

looked about as if he were searching for something he'd lost. Then he found the priest's eyes.

At that moment, as their eyes met, Leopold Swift passed into God's care.

57

By five o'clock in the morning the frogs stopped pitching their appeals for love to prospective mates.

Edward unzipped the door to our tent and sniffed the air, as he always did, a kind of ritual for him. The fresh scent of the woods. Then he took a deep, appreciative breath; he never took these things for granted. The rain had washed the world clean, and the air was sweet with the smell of desert-crested wheatgrass, sagebrush, shooting star, Inyo buckwheat, spiny hop sage, juniper, knobcone pine—a stew of smells. The morning light had not yet crested the mountain.

We'd forgotten, my husband and I, the cries for help during the predawn hours, which in the present circumstances seemed unreal and incongruous—all was perfect in the world. We were aware, of course, that everything—life's worries, the day's travails—always seems worse in the darkest predawn hours, but once the sun rises, those problems evaporate and seem barely worth mentioning. Still, Edward and I carefully searched the vicinity of our campsite, just to be certain.

Edward found them first. They were ensconced under a stony outcropping—Leo with his head resting on Father Tom's leg, seemingly asleep, and Father Tom looking up sleepily, in an odd way, with his upper teeth biting his lower lip. Perhaps he was trying to remember something, or he was confused, I thought at the time. (Later on, Father Tom told me that he had been experiencing what he self-diagnosed as an early stage of dementia: forgetting little things, like where he'd placed his car keys, or bigger things, like some of the words to prayers during mass. He claims that since that terrifying night, his dementia has worsened.)

I stayed with Father Tom and Leo Swift while Edward jogged off, heading down the trail to get help. It took a couple of hours before he made a cell phone call to the Inyo County Sheriff's Office, telling them that one man had probably died and another was injured.

Once the rescuers determined the target area, they immediately initiated search operations. The sheriff department's search-and-rescue team, whose job is to hasten the recovery of lost, injured, or stranded individuals in Inyo and Kings Canyon parks, sent trained personnel bearing appropriate equipment and medical supplies.

The climbing field teams were assembled at the trailhead. There was no safe spot where a helicopter could land, so the men on the ground tackled the trails, lugging heavy first-aid and other emergency supplies on their backs. Two climbing rangers were dispatched to make a quick ascent, while the advanced climbing rescue team of Camille Rose and Taylor Hudson departed the parking lot near the campgrounds adjacent to North Lake. A second team of five climbing rangers also assembled at the campground. They carried extra supplies and prepared to support the advance team for a ground evacuation.

58

Paul and Chandler awakened to the sound of the ladder-backed woodpecker ratta-tapping a hole into lodgepole bark. The morning breeze was chilly, and they huddled together for warmth. Paul's face was buried in the wild tangle of her hair.

The treetops tumbled and tossed.

"We should hit the trail," Paul said, sitting up in the seat.

"I have to pee," she said. There was an Andy Gump porta potty at one end of the parking lot.

She sighed. Her eyebrows went down.

"Chandler, what's wrong?" he said.

"I'm scared."

"Of what?"

"Finding him."

"Your dad? That's what you want, isn't it?"

"This may sound crazy. I don't know. I'm not sure. What if he doesn't want to have anything to do with me?" she said, looking at nothing in particular through the car window. "I mean, I don't think I've thought this through. I mean, what do I say?"

"You say, 'I'm your daughter.' Then you let things play out. Know what I mean? Just let things happen."

She didn't answer.

The sound of the woodpecker's rat-a-tat burrowing for termites suddenly stopped. The morning's serenity was broken when the rescue team arrived. They set up base operations in the unoccupied parking spaces.

59

I was greatly relieved when Edward finally made it back, short of breath. He'd stopped smoking twenty years ago, but I suspect that his lungs are permanently damaged. Moreover, he's fifty-eight years old and beginning to exhibit myriad telltale signs of aging—which is okay, since I'm getting old myself.

Edward brought with him Chandler and Paul, who had inquired about the rescue operation. A description of the two injured men was enough to convince them to follow his lead.

When Chandler and Paul arrived at the site, the two leaders of the crew, who had arrived well ahead of them, were applying CPR on Leo despite the apparent hopelessness of their efforts. They used instant cold packs to ice the injured area of Father Tom's leg and ease swelling, then they compressed the injury by gently wrapping it with an elastic bandage. Because he appeared dehydrated and suffering from hypothermia, they started an IV.

While my husband and I watched and the two medics turned their attention to Father Tom, who appeared to be in a state of shock, Chandler broke away from Paul. In the commotion of the moment, I turned to look at the young man. He is undeniably handsome, with loads of charisma, and I understood immediately why Chandler was attracted to him. The expression on his face, as he watched Chandler's every move, was one of pure concern.

Chandler crouched down beside her father, resting her knees in the dirt. His eyes were now closed, and he seemed to be asleep.

She cradled her father's head in her arms.

The two men stopped their work, and they watched—as we all did—as if we were witnessing something hallowed.

Chandler kissed her father's purple, waxy, stone-cold lips: she kissed a man she'd never seen before in her twenty years of life—a stranger.

What happened next, according to Chandler, cannot be corroborated. As any scientist will tell you, without verification, without empirical or measurable evidence, without testing and retesting of unnatural phenomena, without reproducibility and controls, one cannot—and *should* not, as a *scientist,* in spite of the numerous recorded claims by priests who have experienced this phenomenon while giving the sacrament of extreme unction—embrace her claim. Unfortunately, I wasn't close enough to see for myself, so I must take her story with a high level of skepticism. But she has stated unequivocally and with unwavering, passionate conviction that as her tears fell upon her father's face, his eyes opened briefly. He stared into her eyes for what seemed to her like an eternity but must have been only a moment.

But during that moment, her father seemed to recognize her, and she swears that a flicker of a smile graced his face.

And in that moment of her father's momentary resurrection, she felt a gradual lifting of a burden, and she knew then that she no longer needed to cast off her damaged mother, and she knew that she would marry Paul, the good man who had followed her from the sea-level streets of Santa Monica to the 12,000-foot peaks and glistening, desolate lakes of the Eastern Sierras.

60

It was a chilly day, close to the ocean. Father Tom officiated: a full Catholic funeral mass graced with all its liturgical, incense-scented finery — "opening windows into the sacred," as Father Tom would put it. Edward and I attended, sitting directly behind Chandler's mother.

"I was able to get a copy of Doctor Swift's master's thesis on his namesake, Jonathan Swift, which he wrote on the role of the body in *Gulliver's Travels*," the priest told the assembly. "I know that many of the students in this room are familiar with *Gulliver*, as you were required to read this novel at Lofton, I am told."

Moans and nervous chuckles from the pews were audible to everyone.

"Never fear," he continued. "I'm not here to deliver a lecture on that famous novel — that was your teacher's special talent. Anyway, school's out, and I know you don't want to think about your classes. But there was one thing I noticed right away, when I began reading his paper. I thought you would like to know what he wrote. Before the title page. It was a dedication."

At that moment Father Tom reached into his pocket, his hand emerging, clasping a small piece of paper in his fingers from which he read: "To all my future students, whoever and wherever they may be."

He folded the tiny slip of paper carefully, and tucked it away into his pocket. The room went silent. Although the church only seats some three hundred people, close to a thousand showed up, all of them students, staff, faculty from Lofton—the entire school community, even Myra Glick, of all people, who looked chastened when she saw how many students were crying around her. They had to seat people in folding chairs just outside the church entrance, and hundreds of people were forced to stand throughout the service. Father Tom had had loudspeakers hung outside so that everyone could hear.

"Doctor Swift hadn't begun his teaching career yet, but I think he had a clear vision of why he was a student himself, and why he was writing this paper. He had a clear goal in mind. And by having *you* young people, his beloved students, as his destination made the journey of writing his thesis—a colossal venture, mind you—that much easier.

"I am certain, based on the short time I spent with Doctor Swift, he made many friends, and many of them are his students, and they are here in our church today. I consider—he was—my friend too," he said, and then clasped his palms over his eyes, shepherding back emotion.

He was silent for some time.

Then he regained his composure and continued: "But like the angel, who said to the women at the opening of the tomb, 'There is no need for you to be afraid. I know you are looking for Jesus, who was crucified. He is not here, for he has risen, as he said he would. Come and see the place where he lay, then go quickly and tell his disciples, He has risen from the dead and now he is going ahead of you to Galilee; that is where you will see him.'"

The priest sighed deeply. He suddenly appeared very tired, although there were no outward telltale signs of his ordeal in the mountains.

"So I must add that *your* teacher," he said at last, "*your* colleague, *your* friend—is not here. He is out there, in the woods, which he loved."

Afterward, when the timing was right, I sought out Janice, Chandler's mother, and got a chance to talk to her briefly in Monsignor McGillis Hall. She appeared happy and grateful to have her daughter back.

"I'm afraid I messed her up pretty bad," she told me, visibly awkward. All she knew about my role in all this was that I was one of the people who had come upon her Leo "up there." She also knew I'd witnessed something intimate and private about her family; the father of her child had died somewhat ignominiously, in her view. She had kept up with newspaper and TV coverage of the investigation into her ex-husband's alleged activities at Lofton. Lieutenant Alvarado had tracked her down and questioned her—*harassed* her, in her view—about her ex-husband's whereabouts. And still, despite the passage of time since their breakup, she felt conflicting emotions—embarrassment and sadness, perhaps.

In her mind, as far as she was concerned, I knew more about her and her family than she did. I knew more about her life than she felt comfortable sharing. It was awkward. We were like blind dates in the first few moments of meeting each other.

"She seems very happy to see you," I said, hoping to mitigate her visible discomfort. Her response was an uncertain smile and a barely perceptible nod of the head.

Meanwhile, Chandler and Paul agreed to meet with Sister Mary in the rectory afterward. Although they'd both been baptized as infants, they were required to participate in a series of meetings with the nun over a four-week period to discuss spiritual matters: "A process of inquiry," Sister explained. And then, once they felt ready ("moved by the Holy Spirit," as Sister put it), they were to be married, a good month after the funeral, even though Chandler would be visibly pregnant by then and have to wear a carefully tailored wedding dress.

61

When the date arrived, Father Tom presided over the wedding. It was a small gathering, joyful, in sharp contrast to the funeral, but nevertheless a full Mass. Edward and I attended, of course; so did Janice, who walked her daughter down the aisle. I was surprised to catch sight of Father Ralph; he'd only met Chandler for a few minutes outside the Lofton cafeteria. Headmaster Lubitch was there too, and this impressed me, for I had suspected, wrongly so, that he was simply an administrator and nothing more. But it turns out he is a compassionate educator first and foremost—he spoke highly of Leo's teaching and confirmed that his students adored him.

I spotted Lieutenant Alvarado, seated in the last pew. He told me in private after the ceremony that they'd closed the case on Leo and he was glad because "Buddhism has no concept of sin" and he'd made it his business to "reserve judgment" until all the facts of the case were in—which would never happen. The lieutenant seemed more than happy to elaborate: "You see, you have to *understand.* The Buddha explains that it is in *not* understanding, in *not* realizing the nature of existence, that beings tangle themselves in troubles in the world."

There were three readings, the first of them from the Old Testament. After the gospel reading, Father Tom gave a homily drawn from the sacred text and peppered it with nature imagery, as he almost always did. He spoke about the mystery of Christian marriage and the dignity of wedded love. Then came the exchanging of vows, the Liturgy of the Eucharist, Communion prayers, the concluding rite, the final blessing, Holy Communion, closing prayers.

But what I remember most were Chandler's tears of gratitude.

Epilogue

Edward, my husband, usually remains dispassionate about his work. He's learned to keep his emotions in check when collecting and recording in the wild. "Otherwise I might muck up the data," he reasons. This diligent objectivity is one of the many things I love about him. He counterbalances my tendency to what he calls (rather pejoratively) "spiritualize" my work, whatever that means. What I think he means is that I approach science from an emotional perspective. "You should be an artist. Maybe a writer," he often tells me. However, as detached and objective as he claims he is, lately Edward has been consumed by melancholy. Because of the frogs.

I think of myself—and I say this with conscious humility, for I know too well my shortcomings—as an artistic scientist, or a scientific artist. Either way, I suppose I view the world in more elegiac terms than Edward. My method of scientific inquiry is no different,

I feel, than Picasso's experiments in cubism or Monet's studies of haystacks in different seasons. You get an idea, and you explore it. For example, Karl von Frisch—who proved through painstaking observation that the figure-eight dance of the honey bee is a sophisticated form of communication and that a successful forager can signal to other bees in the colony information regarding the direction and distance to nectar-yielding flowers—was not that different from Antonio Canova, who could gaze at a block of white Carrera marble, visualize Cupid and Psyche, and chip away at it until the two lovers emerge, wings and all. Or a poet who, like an alchemist, transmutes word imagery from the netherworld into mental gold.

I lost my mother when I was eight, to ovarian cancer, and my dad when I was twenty-four, to cirrhosis of the liver, and I suppose these events define me to a certain extent. They, at least, have helped shape me. Dad and I parted ways when I left for college to study biology, and I never saw him again. As far as I'm concerned, I am an orphan.

But the wilderness, sublime spirit, Mother Nature— my adopted mother—can also be fatal, I know. As a scientist working in the mountains, I'm well aware that the green world can be anything but "nurturing" at times; the sun cares little for the victories and losses of human beings below, and predators often kill with impunity: "Nature, red in tooth and claw," as Tennyson put it. God's creatures—frogs and waterbugs, starfish and manta rays, marmots and black bears—are not like us. They do not kill because they seek revenge for being betrayed, or act out of hatred, or envy, or feelings of sinfulness. They kill only to stay alive, to nourish themselves, to protect themselves or their young, and because it is in their DNA to do so.

So let it be known. I am a scientist. And yet I believe in miracles. How can this be? Even Christians today— for many of them, the age of miracles belongs to the early church. For me, however, phenomena that defy logical explanation and render me silent can only be described as miracles—and I experience these things all the time when I'm hiking the Sierras. I am well aware that miracles violate the laws of nature. I get it. But I'm sure I witnessed one transpire high up there near Desolation Lake.

Edward and I love exploring the natural world; working in the woods with amphibians is our religion. We find miracles aplenty in the Sierras. I think Albert Einstein said it best: "There are only two ways to live your life. One is as though nothing is a miracle. The other is as though everything is a miracle."

But now we're back in our cozy little home—a one-bedroom, one-bath, ranch-style house in town. As I finish this writing, it's winter and unusually cold outside, although the snowpack in the high Sierras is dangerously low this year.

Edward and I never returned to Humphreys Basin; we'd finished our work there. In any case, there are other areas in the region in which the *Rana muscosa* species is threatened with extinction, and we will venture out again in the spring to do our best to help save them.

For now, it's time to put another conifer log on the fire.

Dr. Sylvia Henestry
California Department of Forestry
Bishop, California
January 16, 2019

CPSIA information can be obtained
at www.ICGtesting.com
Printed in the USA
BVHW040215020519
547187BV00013B/143/P

9 780578 470177